Cry of Dragons

(Elves, Drelves & Dragons Book Three)

C. Star

Dedication

Dedicated to my readers.

Thank you for following me on this fantastical journey!

Strap in for another wild ride.

www.Cstarbooks.com

Don't miss the first two books in the trilogy!

Book One and Two of Elves, Drelves & Dragons

Table of Contents

The three
Realms
Drelf Kingdom
Dragon Graveyard
Larimar Falls
The Arden
Shrouded Vale
Monrovia River
Elf Kingdom
Rivenmoor
Nylia River
Fae Bridge
Dragon Kingdom

Prologue

Long before ruin scarred the realms, before trust burned to ash, there was balance.

Elves and dragons once walked in accord beneath the Great Covenant—a bond forged in honor and sealed in truth. White dragons, guardians of the sky, stood beside the elves who protected the forests below. Fire and leaf. Strength and wisdom. A harmony that shaped the world.

But pride breeds deceit.

And somewhere between pride and silence, something fractured.

The Covenant did not shatter in a single blow. It cracked in whispers. In fear unspoken. In love denied. In truths buried too quickly to be named.

From that fracture came exile.

From exile, division.

And from division, a species born between realms.

When dragons turned from one another, their scales remembered.

When elves chose fear over understanding, their forests remembered.

But when blood once joined was cast out, the world remembered most of all.

So the white dragons wove a warning into the bones of time:

When the realms stand again upon the edge—

when fear disguises itself as mercy—

marks will rise where once there was division.

It was not a promise.

It was a warning.

Ages passed, and the first mark awakened, burned upon a drelf descended from the outcast line. Through her, hope flickered again. Through her, the balance tilted toward the light.

But balance never stays still.

A second mark followed, claimed in silence by an elf. When it blazed to life, its power shook the realms.

And the world answered.

A battle erupted as giants fell and blood soaked the Arden. Flame and shadow warred beneath a sky torn open by dragons.

When the storm ended, ash drifted like gray snow across the forest floor, softening death and ruin. The giants withdrew with silent steps, carrying Gravorn, their fallen leader. Their oath to the elves had been fulfilled.

Beneath burned roots, the Shadow Panthers prowled, finishing what flame had begun. The Arden fed upon itself once more.

But beneath that silence, something else was rising.

And the realms, trembling on the brink, would soon learn that when dragons cry, the world listens...

Chapter 1

Sickly yellow eyes snapped open.

Pain seared through his body— broken ribs, scorched wings, blood caked beneath shattered scales. A mountain of ruin lay atop him.

But none of that mattered.

Because he was alive.

Drakor's talons flexed, gouging into the ash-soaked ground as he clawed upward.

Rock split. Bone shifted. He dragged his battered frame through the wreckage, snarling with each breath. At last, he heaved himself free, wings hanging in torn ribbons at his sides as he shook ash and dirt from his molted green scales, each movement sending small avalanches sliding off his twisted body.

His eyes swept the surrounding ruins. Smoke curled upward through broken stone and shattered roots. The stench of death seeped into his nostrils, thick and cloying. He inhaled deeply.

"Yes..." he snarled, voice like gravel and flame. "Dead. All of them."

Drakor limped forward, each step sending knives of pain lancing through his ribs. His wings dragged behind him, scorched membranes tearing against the stone.

But he did not slow.

Pain was irrelevant.

Survival was not.

He prowled through the burned debris, talons scraping blackened earth. His nostrils flared. His tongue tasted the air.

There.

The scent of dragon blood.

Not his own.

He followed it through the devastation until the ground dipped sharply into a massive crater carved into the forest floor, wide as a lake. The place where Zyressa had fallen.

Blackened trees slumped inward around it. Rocks split from the force. The soil itself had melted to glass beneath dragonfire. Drakor stared down into the hollow, breath hissing through his teeth. The crater was empty. There was no charred body. No bones. Nothing but soot.

But the earth still hummed from the violence of her impact.

A low growl vibrated in his throat. "She should be here," he rasped. "I saw her fall."

His tail lashed, scattering shards of glasslike stone.

He inhaled again, determined, desperate. "If she lives..." he whispered, voice thick with pain and fury, "...I will find her."

He tried to spread his wings, but agony ripped through him, white-hot and blinding. His legs buckled. He collapsed against the charred ground, ash billowing around him. His ribs ground with every labored breath.

Snarling, Drakor dragged himself forward, talons gouging furrows in the melted earth, pulling his ruined body along.

He would heal.

And when his strength returned, he would tear the truth from the world.

If Zyressa had crawled back from death, he would find her. She would seek the power of the second mark, and the elf who bore it.

The mark belonged to him.

And he would take it—or destroy everything to claim it.

The war-torn group of elves and drelves spilled into the thin morning light, dust and ash clinging to clothes, scales, boots, and padded feet. Their breaths came ragged from clawing their way out of the collapsed tunnel.

Caelith limped forward, Master Trainer Aldareth bracing him with one steady arm while holding the reins of their horses in the other, Aldareth's dark gelding snorting at the acrid air, Caelith's horse shifting anxiously beside him.

Zeynar leaned against the trunk of a blackened tree, drawing slow, steadying breaths. His wings, torn and singed at the edges, trembled from strain. But they had worked when it mattered most, lifting him clear of the final collapse by inches.

Aelar emerged next, blood dried against his temple, one arm held tight to his ribs. His horse nudged him insistently, sensing his pain.

Erynder and Seliora took their places at the flanks, bows half-drawn, eyes sweeping the forest for threats that might still be lurking.

Steel, Thalendir's black stallion, tossed his head and stamped, nerves taut. Silverwind and Embermane paced beside him, ears pricked toward the silent treeline. Thalendir had rescued the horses on the way into the tunnels, knowing Eldrin and Finnian would rather die than abandon their mounts.

The forest was quiet, too quiet, its natural hum muted beneath a heavy, expectant stillness that settled over them like fog.

Finnian rubbed at the silver lines burning on his temples, the fresh mark pulsing like a heartbeat beneath his skin. It should have been Eldrin, he thought. Not me. I never wanted this.

Lyria stood pale and unsteady, leaning against the rock face. The mark on her neck flickered in the same rhythm as Finnian's. She glanced toward him. He felt it too, the confusion, the questions, the fear that came with being chosen.

Kaelis hovered close, wings tight and protective. One eye flicked toward Finnian, and her jaw tightened. *What am I supposed to do with this one?* she wondered.

She was a drelf. He was an elf.

And he was now marked.

Her own words to Lyria from days before boomeranged back at her now: *Elves are our en-e-my.*

Years of mistrust, of scorn, separation, and centuries of wounds, crowded in on her all at once. And now, to make things worse, Lyria no longer remembered the elf, Eldrin. The one they had all risked their lives to save. The one Kaelis had hated at first.

She should be glad about it. She had, after all, accused Lyria of betraying the drelves for him. But she was not glad. Not even a little.

Confusion twisted in her chest, sharp and unwelcome. About her own situation... and now, about Lyria's. Nothing felt simple anymore. Everything felt tangled. And Kaelis hated tangled things.

Eldrin stood a short distance from the others, shoulders tense, ash streaked across his face like war paint. His sword hung at his side, but it was the dagger, the blade still in his hand, that held him motionless.

He stared down at it as though something might have etched answers along its edge. He turned it slowly, feeling the familiar weight settle into his palm. The hilt molded to his grip as though it recognized him, as though it had chosen him long before. It understood him and answered him.

He had grown up believing the dagger belonged to his father, King Eldermyst. A symbol of duty. Of the legacy he would uphold. The king had given it to him on his coming-of-age birthday, placing it in his hands with quiet pride. "Carry it with honor," he had said. Eldrin had thought the weight he felt was responsibility.

But later... Gantar had told him the truth. The blade had not been his father's.

It had been his mother's.

Thariel. The mother whose memory lived in flashes of warmth and shadowed loss. Eldrin could still recall her touch on his shoulder when she spoke to him, soft but steady. He could almost smell the faint trace of lavender that clung to her clothes. And he remembered the quiet way she always hummed before she sang, as if catching the melody from the very air.

Her songs still lived on in him. War hymns that thrummed like a heartbeat.

Lullabies that had eased his nightmares, and songs woven with ancient magic, though he had not understood that then.

He remembered how she smiled when she taught him to hold a blade.

“Balance, Eldrin,” she would whisper, hands guiding his. “A weapon mirrors the soul. Listen, and it will speak.”

And now, as he held her dagger, he knew she had spoken through it long before he was born. The hilt warmed against his palm, as if her memory, her strength, lived inside the metal.

It hollowed him. Even now, even with her gone, he felt her presence. And as long as he held the blade, some part of her still walked beside him.

The Aetherstone at his hip pulsed faintly, soft, steady, alive, echoing the ache gathering beneath his ribs. He barely felt the bruises beneath his armor or the sting of cuts along his arms. The only thing he felt, truly felt, was the hollow place his mother had first left behind... and now that hollow place deepened by the drelf standing before him, who looked at him as if he were no one at all.

His gaze flicked to his brother, Thalendir's soot-streaked face, Steel's restless stamping, and a familiar knot tightened in his chest. Thalendir had saved the horses, rallied the elves, carved their path through shadow and ruin.

Once again, the heir had done everything right.

All Eldrin had done was drop the dagger instead of driving it into Camyra's dark heart. It had been Finnian who had struck the killing blow. Finnian, who had saved him, saved them all, and now bore the second mark on his temples.

But none of that mattered. Because the only thing that mattered stood just a few paces away.

His eyes found Lyria.

The drelf he had rescued from the nemods in the Enchanted Forest. The one he had committed treason for. The one who had leapt after him into the Abyss in the Dragon Graveyard. The same one who had surrendered his memory so he could live.

And she stood there now as though she had never seen him before.

Eldrin swallowed hard. The Aetherstone throbbed once more, echoing the tremor in his chest. He wanted to speak. Wanted to cross the distance between them. Wanted to remind her of everything they had survived, everything they had been.

Instead, he stepped forward, quietly, almost cautiously, as though approaching a wound that might tear wider if he moved too fast.

"Are you hurt?" he asked softly.

Lyria stiffened. Her gaze lifted to his, those amethyst eyes he had carried through fire and nightmare, and something inside Eldrin cracked open.

But there was no recognition.

No spark.

No warmth.

"Please," Lyria said quietly, instinctively stepping back. "I'm trying to remember you. But I just... don't."

Kaelis moved instantly, sliding into place between them. Her stare sharpened, but her voice stayed soft. "Take a breath, Eldrin."

"I'm trying," he whispered, throat tight.

Lyria's brows knit, confusion flickering across her face. She looked at him like a stranger, like someone he could no longer reach.

It struck harder than any blade.

Finnian dragged a hand through his hair. "Lyria, he—,"

"Don't." Eldrin lifted a hand to stop him. His voice was steady, but only barely. "Let her be."

Lyria swallowed, wings twitching faintly. "I remember him," she said, pointing to Finnian. "And that one," she added, nodding toward Thalendir. "But you..." She hesitated, searching his face. "I don't."

The Aetherstone throbbed softly at Eldrin's side, echoing the hollow ache inside him.

Kaelis exhaled, her voice barely above a whisper. "Maybe... with time, you'll remember giving up his memory to the Tree Sage. And that you risked everything for him."

Lyria blinked. No memory surfaced. Only bewilderment.

Eldrin closed his eyes.

Finnian cleared his throat, his voice a rough attempt at levity. "You two were pretty dramatic together," he muttered. "Lots of heroics. Lots of tension. A ridiculous amount of staring."

Lyria shot him a baffled look.

Kaelis elbowed him. Gently.

Eldrin lifted his head, meeting Lyria's gaze once more. "It's all right," he breathed. "You don't have to remember me."

His voice softened. "Because I won't forget you. And I'll help you remember."

A beat.

"If you want to."

She looked away. His eyes felt like they pierced straight through her, and she felt... nothing. Or almost nothing.

“Maybe...” she whispered.

Chapter 2

Darkness shifted like a living thing, coiling, tightening, reclaiming shape as though the Abyss itself exhaled. For centuries, this hollow had remained undisturbed. Until now.

A tremor rippled through the chamber, small at first, like the rustle of wings somewhere deep within the stone. Then deeper. Older. A pulse that did not belong to the Abyss alone.

Vartharax inhaled, the sound like stone grinding against stone. "No..."

Covenant magic did not strike. It closed around him.

Smoldering embers flared along his scales, each pulse of heat revealing more of the black dragon's vast, serpentine form: wings folded like mountains, claws half-buried in volcanic rock, tail coiled in forced stillness. Chains of ancient power ignited, runes burning as they locked into place, binding scale and sinew alike.

The dark ruler of the Abyss did not move. He could not. The light held him, woven strands clinging to his body like molten brands. The power he once commanded slammed against the barrier, straining like a starved beast snapping at iron.

Darkness thickened, furious and denied.

A low rumble vibrated deep in his chest. "Another chosen..."

A guttural sound tore from him, long, violent, earth-shattering.

ROOOAAAR...

The ground felt it and trembled. The surrounding air recoiled. It tore through the realm of darkness.

And beyond it, elves stopped, drelves froze, and dragons listened.

The old elf sage had not slept. Not truly. Not since King Eldermyst's command echoed through the war room: *See that they return. Both of them.*

Those words clung to him now as he walked the dim corridor of the elf kingdom. The Aetherstone pendant at his throat emitted a faint glow that brushed the stone walls with trembling light.

They had sent four spies into the Arden, some of their best. Charged with bringing back word of the king's sons. Charged with doing whatever was necessary to find them.

But they had not yet returned.

Outside, dawn had begun its slow climb through the gray mist that settled over their land and clung to it like breath on a dying flame. Ever since Eldrin and Thalendir vanished into the Arden, clouds had draped the kingdom, and light barely broke through.

Gantar reached the open archway that overlooked the kingdom below, the place where elven kings had stood for thousands of years to survey their realm. The air was wrong. It was too still. As if the world itself had been holding its breath since the first mark appeared.

He closed his eyes. The Aetherstone pulsed once against his chest, slow, steady, warm. Then once more, sharper this time.

Gantar stiffened. "Not again..." he whispered, more to himself than to the stone.

The Aetherstone had only ever behaved this way twice: the night Thariel died, when the stone had passed into his hands, and again when the first mark awakened on Lyria Ironwing.

His fingers tightened on the carved railing until his knuckles blanched. "The second mark..." he breathed. "It has chosen."

He closed his eyes, and a face rose behind them, temples lit with silver fire.

An elf with more heart than sense, more loyalty than caution. A young warrior utterly unprepared for the weight now tied to him.

A soft breath escaped the sage's lips. "Finnian," he murmured.

The balance had shifted. Two marks, one prophecy. One now rested with the elves, and one with the drelves, tipping the scale, however slightly, toward the light.

But this was no end. This was a beginning.

Gantar straightened as a wind stirred, carrying the scent of ash and distant pine. Somewhere far below, a horn sounded, the elf watch beginning their shift. Life moved on, as it always did. But something beneath it all was shifting.

He felt it in the ripple of the leaves. In the faint tremor threading through the world's breath and in the Aetherstone's nervous pulse, like a heartbeat slipping out of time. As if the boundary between life and death had thinned.

Then the sound came.

It rolled through him, long, languid, immense, too vast to be heard so much as felt.

It pressed against his senses, against the stone beneath his hand, against the breath in his chest. Gantar's fingers tightened on the Aetherstone. He knew what it was the instant the roar tore through the realms. A chill raced up his spine.

Because he knew darkness the world had not known in ages was answering the light.

Not rising with it, but rising because of it.

And it was hungry.

"What worries you, my friend?"

King Eldermyst's voice startled Gantar.

The sage turned, robes whispering against the stone as he faced the king. Eldermyst stood framed in the archway's soft glow, his silver hair catching what little light filtered through the mist. He looked older today, shadows carved deeper along his jaw, the faint lines beside his eyes more pronounced. But his posture remained steady, regal and commanding.

Still, Gantar saw the tension in his shoulders, the strain of too many nights with too little hope. "Forgive me, my king," Gantar said quietly. "I did not hear you approach."

"That alone tells me something is amiss," Eldermyst replied, stepping up beside him. He clasped his hands behind his back, his gaze sweeping the fog-draped valley. "You have walked these corridors for centuries and never once failed to sense my presence."

Gantar hesitated.

Eldermyst's eyes narrowed, not with anger, but with concern. "Tell me."

"The second mark has awakened," Gantar murmured.

The king stilled. For a heartbeat, the mist itself seemed to quiet, hovering around them as if listening. "And has it chosen someone?" Eldermyst asked, voice tight.

"Yes," Gantar said, with hesitation.

The king inhaled sharply. "One of my sons?"

"No, my king. It has chosen another."

The king let out a long sigh. Relief washed over his face as a long silence fell.

Then, softly, disbelievingly, Gantar whispered, "Finnian."

The king's brows drew together, not in anger, but in confusion. "Finnian," he repeated softly. "Eldrin's friend?"

Gantar inclined his head. "A brave young elf," the sage said quietly. "Loyal. Fierce of heart. But not prepared for the burden the mark demands."

Eldermyst exhaled a slow, measured breath. Relief washed over him, and his shoulders relaxed as if someone had lifted an enormous weight off him.

"So, the power meant to guide the realms," Eldermyst murmured, "has chosen a warrior who never sought it."

"Power rarely chooses the ones who seek it," Gantar replied.

The king's gaze drifted to the valley again as the mist shifted like breath between distant trees. "And my sons?" he asked quietly. "Does the stone sense them?"

Gantar closed his eyes. "Your sons are safe... for now," He answered. "But the stone is uneasy. The balance trembles. And whatever chose Finnian..."

His voice frayed into a whisper. "...something else cries in answer."

Eldermyst's jaw tightened, the muscles along his cheek flexing like tempered steel. "Like what?"

Gantar turned toward the king. The morning mist curled between them like a living thing, thin, searching, almost sentient. "Darkness," he breathed. "Older than the dark elves. Older than prophecy itself. And hungry."

Eldermyst swallowed. "And it cries out because two marks now belong to the light?"

"Light never rises without summoning shadow," Gantar murmured. "Balance demands it."

An icy wind swept across the balcony, tugging at their cloaks. The king shivered, not from the cold.

Gantar lowered his gaze. The wind shifted again. Deep within the misted valley, a raven shrieked. Both elves stilled. They did not need to speak.

The Aetherstone's cold flicker deepened, answering the king's dread with a silence heavier than any words. A storm was gathering, older than their ancestors, older than their kingdoms, older even than the Covenant.

And its shadow was already falling upon the realms.

Chapter 3

The Arden was talking. Not with birdsong or life, but with a sound, a cry that slithered through the trees and crawled along the ground beneath their feet. The elves and the drelves felt it before they heard it.

A pressure in the chest. A tremor in the bones. A warning that had no words.

The forest stilled. Branches froze mid-sway. Ash hung unmoving in the air. Even the wind seemed to recoil, as if the Arden itself were holding its breath. No one spoke or reached for a weapon. They looked at one another, elf to drelf, rider to winged shadow, not asking what it was, but whether the others had felt it too.

And then the silence returned, heavier than before. But the Arden did not exhale.

Maybe they had imagined it. Maybe it was only the echo of battle, ringing in their ears, fading too slowly.

Lyria lifted a hand to her throat, fingers brushing the mark burning there. Across from her, Finnian went still. Two fingers rose instinctively to the mark on his temples as their eyes met. No words passed between them, but she knew he had felt it too. Something deep. Vast and hungry. It was not wind, memory, or imagination.

There was no mistaking its source. A dragon stirred.

Another faint tremor ran beneath their feet. Not enough to spark panic, but enough that every elf and drelf lifted their heads at once, instincts snapping to attention. Caelith froze mid-step. Aldareth's hand went to his sword. Zeynar's wings twitched as a shiver cut through the air. Even the horses felt it, stamping, tossing their heads, snorting uneasily.

There was no denying it this time. Deep within the underworld, a dragon cried out.

Thalendir had been watching his brother standing before the drelf with silver wings, heart practically in his hands. And she had looked at him as if he were nothing. She did not even remember him. Thalendir's jaw tightened.

Of course she didn't. *That's a drelf for you. Never trust one. Not with your kingdom. Not with your life, or with your brother's heart.* He had said as much before. Shouted it, even. And now, here was proof.

He shifted his grip on Steel's reins, fingers curling with a frustration so old it tasted bitter. Eldrin had always led with his heart, impulsive, reckless, loyal long past reason. And here he stood again, wounded in ways a blade would never reach.

Idiot, Thalendir thought, not unkindly, but sharply, painfully. *He'll hand his heart to anyone with a wounded wing.*

Yet Thalendir's gaze slid to Lyria. She looked fragile, pale, barely standing, but unbroken. She had come for them. Risked her life. Fought dragons to save his brother. All true. But the look on Eldrin's face, a crack carved straight through him, made something twist in Thalendir's chest, something he did not want to name.

So he hardened himself instead. She didn't remember him. *Good.* Maybe this time his brother would finally stop handing trust to creatures who didn't deserve it.

He straightened, eyes narrowing toward the shadowed trees. Then, without a word, he crossed the distance to Eldrin and held out the reins. "We need to get moving."

Eldrin didn't reach for them. His eyes flicked past Thalendir toward Lyria, not with accusation, not even with hope, but with the stunned ache of someone trying to understand how a world could shift beneath his feet in a single breath.

Thalendir followed his gaze, jaw tightening. "Eldrin," he said more firmly, lowering his voice so only his brother heard, "this place is not safe."

Thalendir held the reins out again, this time with urgency threaded through his voice. "Take her, brother," he murmured. "Before whatever is out there... decides we are on the menu."

Eldrin swallowed, the ache burning all the way down. Then, slowly, he reached for the reins. He closed his eyes for a single breath. When he opened them again, something had shifted. Not healed, or steadied, but braced.

He took the reins from Thalendir, his grip firm despite the tremor beneath his skin. "You're right," he said quietly. "It's time to leave this place."

Thalendir studied him for a moment, surprised, perhaps even a little proud, then dipped his head once. "Good," he said. "Now let's move."

Eldrin turned away before the ache could resurface, leading Silverwind forward as resolve settled, hard-won, across his shoulders.

Finnian watched him swing into the saddle, too forceful, too sharp. He knew the signs. Eldrin was not giving up. Just redirecting. Re-anchoring. Doing what Eldrin had always done best.

Finnian exhaled.

Of course, Eldrin would not abandon Lyria, mark or no mark, memory or no memory. But something else had risen behind his eyes now. Duty to his kingdom and royal bloodline. A prince again, whether or not he wanted it.

Chapter 4

Drakor had dragged himself into a narrow cave carved into the cliffside deep within the Arden, its mouth half-hidden behind ivy that twisted like snakes around smoke-stained stone. Every breath scraped across broken ribs. The air tasted of damp rock, crushed leaves, blood... and something older, an echo of magic clinging to the walls like a stain.

Darkness pressed in from all sides, not vast or echoing like the Abyss, but tight. Constricting. A hollow barely large enough for his battered frame. Here, carved into the bones of the forest, he lay curled in pain.

His wings hung in torn strips. Scales cracked and blackened as his body trembled under its own weight. But he pushed the pain aside. Pain was familiar. It meant survival, and that he was alive. And alive meant dangerous.

He lowered his head to the cold stone, letting the cave swallow his labored breaths. Outside, the forest lay silent, too silent. Even the panthers had moved on, and the shadows seemed to hold their breath.

Drakor closed his eyes. As he lay in the narrow dark, something stirred, something beneath the world, something distant but unmistakable. A tremor. Faint at first, like the shiver of a dying flame. Then deeper, older. A pulse that did not belong to the forest, or to any living creature above the ground.

Drakor stiffened, claws sinking into the cold stone as he felt another pulse from below.

From the Abyss. His breath hitched, and his eyes widened, pupils narrowing to slits. "...Master?"

The cavern shuddered, dust drifting from the ceiling. A ripple of ancient power threaded through the walls, cold, oppressive, unmistakable.

Vartharax. But not as he had been. This was weaker. He was bound, yet seething with hunger. Even in his broken state, the call coiled around Drakor's mind like smoke.

He lowered his head to the stone, trembling. "You... are bound," he rasped.

The cavern flickered with a faint, unnatural glow, the echo of Vartharax's power bleeding through the cracks of creation. A spark returned to Drakor's eyes. Small. Dangerous. Enough to make him forget the pain and smile.

The realms had no master now. This was his moment at last. "Yes..." he whispered. "The world will soon learn who truly rules the darkness."

The company pressed on. Eldrin kept to the front of the group, Silverwind picking her steps carefully across the scorched ground. Every line of him was carved with quiet resolve, the pain buried, or perhaps tightly leashed.

Thalendir rode just to his left, Steel's hooves striking sparks on stone as the stallion tossed his head, ears pinned at the unnatural silence.

Finnian stayed close on Eldrin's other side. The silver lines on his temples glowed faintly, pulsing to a rhythm only he could feel. He tried to ignore it, but the mark had its own heartbeat now.

Above them, the drelves took to the air. Their wings unfurled with soft, rhythmic snaps. Kaelis and Zeynar flew highest, scouting the path ahead. Two younger drelves swept low, circling protectively around the company.

And Lyria flew alone, behind them all. Her silver wings carried her steadily, but not without strain. Exhaustion gripped her bones; the battle had taken its toll on every one of them. But something else pulled at her, something heavier than fatigue. Her thoughts and confusion over the elf. Eldrin. The name whispered through her mind like a half-remembered dream. A story told to her by someone else. A memory dipped in shadow, unreachable no matter how she strained for it.

Had she really risked her life for an elf?

Her wings faltered a fraction, just enough for Kaelis to glance back sharply. Lyria steadied herself, jaw tightening. The others remembered. The world remembered. But she did not. And that frightened her more than any battle ever had.

The mist thinned as they climbed, but the silence did not. The Arden loomed behind them like a sleeping beast, its charred branches clawing at the pale sky. Every so often, someone glanced back, unable to shake the feeling that the forest watched them leave.

Trees gave way to jagged stone outcroppings and stretches of wind-scoured earth. The smell of ash faded into the frigid mountain air. Eldrin slowed Silverwind as the terrain steepened. Thalendir raised a hand, signaling the others to halt.

Ahead, the ridge rose like a broken spine, the boundary between wood and wasteland. Beyond it, a faint gray haze drifted upward like breath from something buried. And below... the Dragon Graveyard, where even the wind refused to cross that threshold.

Kaelis and Zeynar descended in tight spirals, landing lightly on the rocks beside Eldrin. Their wings twitched, uneasy. The group stood together on the slope, elves and drelves, winged shadows and steel, looking down at the skeletal remains where countless dragons had fallen, where magic pooled thick and dangerous beneath the bones of the world.

Finnian's temples pulsed once, a sharp flash of silver that made him wince. Lyria drifted down from the air, landing a few paces behind the others. Her wings folded tight against her back, her gaze fixed on the graveyard below, on the place where she had died. And lived again.

A shiver moved through the company. Behind them lay a forest that had nearly swallowed them whole. Below them waited a valley haunted by memory and bones.

Eldrin tightened his grip on Silverwind's reins. They had not discussed what would happen when they reached the divide. No one dared to. But the moment stood before them now, carved into the earth like a wound that refused to close.

One trail wound upward toward the jagged peaks marking the path to the Drelf Kingdom. The other dipped toward Larimar Falls, the Enchanted Forest, and home, back to everything the elves had left behind. Duty. Family. Expectation.

Thalendir exhaled, the sound sharp in the cold air. "I guess this is it," he said. "Time for us to go our merry ways."

No one moved. No one agreed. Because nothing about this parting felt merry.

Zeynar folded his wings and stepped nearer, his gaze flicking between the brothers. Kaelis hovered just behind Lyria, her eyes darting toward Finnian. The weary elves and torn-winged drelves surrounding them shifted uneasily, waiting for someone to speak first.

Eldrin's knuckles whitened on the reins. He looked at Lyria, really looked, and the ache threatened to return. The memory she didn't have. The bond she didn't feel.

Then he looked at Thalendir. His brother, and future king. The one who expected him to ride home, stand before their father, and act as though none of this had changed him. A long breath left Eldrin's chest. He didn't want to part ways. Not like this.

Finnian eased his horse up beside him and straightened in the saddle, the silver at his temples flickering faintly. "After everything that's happened..." he said.

His gaze slid to Lyria, then to Thalendir, and snagged, just for a heartbeat, on Kaelis. Her blue eyes struck like a spark against snow. "...we can't just leave you."

Silence fell. Not the easy kind. Kaelis shifted her weight, wings rustling, clearly uncomfortable with how close his words landed. Lyria blinked, caught between the tension and a feeling she couldn't name.

All eyes slid back to Finnian as he swallowed. "I mean them," he said quickly, nodding toward the drelves. The words came out fast, too fast, as if he were shoving them past the burn beneath his temples before doubt could catch them.

Master Trainer Aldareth moved his mount forward, his dark horse stepping between the brothers. "The king will expect word of his sons," Aldareth said quietly. "At least some of us should return to the elf kingdom."

Lyria looked at Finnian, then Thalendir. Her gaze skimmed over Eldrin, quickly, carefully, as though merely seeing his pain might reopen something inside her she couldn't name. Silver shimmered along her wings, beautiful, but battered. Her chin lifted, regal despite exhaustion. "I speak for my kingdom," she said, cool, clipped, controlled.

Kaelis stepped closer, arms crossed, posture daring anyone to object.

Lyria looked between them, Thalendir with rigid distrust, Finnian with earnest concern, Kaelis with fierce loyalty. "You owe us nothing more," she said.

Then her gaze brushed Eldrin's face again, searching for something she did not understand. Her voice softened. "But... thank you."

Thalendir sat still, eyes flicking between Eldrin, Finnian, and Lyria. Then a slow, satisfied grin broke across his face. "Well then," he said, nudging Steel forward, "I suppose that answers everything."

Steel stepped forward first. The sound of his hooves on stone was small, too small for what it meant, but it echoed anyway, sharp in the mountain air. Master Aldareth and his elves fell in line, but no one spoke. One by one, the elven riders followed, except Eldrin and Finnian.

Eldrin stayed where he was, watching Thalendir's back as his brother rode ahead, never looking back, shoulders squared, spine straight, every inch the heir returning to duty. Then his gaze drifted to Lyria. She stood with her wings folded tight, chin lifted, eyes fixed on the peaks beyond him, not on the elves descending the mountain path. Not on him. As if looking would cost her something she could not afford to lose. Something twisted in his chest. He had crossed fire and shadow for her, and now he was leaving without even a goodbye.

Finnian held Embermane back, staying with Eldrin. Ahead, Kaelis hovered near Lyria, her posture rigid, her attention forward, but Finnian felt it anyway. The almost look. The hesitation. He opened his mouth and closed it again. Whatever he might have said would only make the leaving harder. So he did what he always did. He smiled, crooked, soft, entirely too brave.

Kaelis did not smile back. She nodded. Then her wings flexed, a door slamming shut. Zeynar watched it all from a few paces back, silent, eyes narrowed, but he said nothing as the space between elf and drelf stretched wider with every step the horses took.

The path ahead split fully now, with nothing but stone and wind between them. Eldrin took one last look over his shoulder. Lyria did not turn around. With a quiet breath, he turned his horse toward the descending trail, and the elves started down the mountain.

Chapter 5

Kaelis flew close to Lyria, never more than a few wing-lengths away. She said nothing, but her sharp gaze tracked every flicker of Lyria's expression. Every pause, every moment her eyes went distant, waiting for any sign she might remember.

Lyria's focus remained on the mountains ahead. Her thoughts turned inward, tangled with half-feelings and shadows of moments she could not grasp. Somewhere behind her ribs, something ached, but it had no name.

Above them, Zeynar circled once, then again, his torn wings carrying him with practiced care. His gaze drifted to Kaelis, how she watched Lyria with unwavering focus, how her attention never strayed. The elf with the easy grin was gone now. *Good.* He had nothing against elves. They had fought bravely enough. But that one had drawn Kaelis's eyes too often. Had pulled at her attention in ways Zeynar did not like.

He adjusted his flight, drawing closer. It was best this way. Elves and drelves did not mix. And it was time they got back to the way things were supposed to be.

The path narrowed as the mountains rose higher. Ahead, the stone spires of the drelf kingdom pierced the clouds, jagged, defiant, alive.

Kaelis exhaled. "We're close."

Lyria beat her tired wings faster at the sight of it. Home. So close she could almost feel the stone beneath her feet again. She was so focused on the rising peaks that she nearly missed it. A flicker of gold drifted across the wind. Not ash, or mist, but light. Her breath caught. And for the first time since the forest, something inside her stirred, warm, bright, achingly familiar.

She would recognize that dust anywhere. It shimmered once, twice, then streaked past her, vanishing downslope, toward the mountain path below.

Lyria turned sharply, scanning the air, expecting to see her little friend. Nothing. Only the fading sparkle... and the uneasy sense that his appearance might not be a good thing.

The last of the elves disappeared down the mountain path, their cloaks swallowed by mist. Finnian eased Embermane up beside Eldrin as the trail widened, his temples faintly glowing, unnoticed in the moment.

"Hey," he murmured, leaning close. "Do you think she misses me?"

Eldrin blinked, the words not quite landing. "What?" he asked.

Finnian glanced around, then lifted a finger behind his hand and pointed discreetly toward the drelf kingdom. "You know..." he whispered, a crooked grin tugging at his mouth.

For the first time since they began the journey, Eldrin smiled, a real one, small and tired, but real. "Finnian," he said, shaking his head, "you are insufferable."

Finnian's grin widened. "Right. Then would you say that's one of my better qualities?"

Eldrin let out a soft, disbelieving laugh. A sudden warmth brushed against his side as the Aetherstone flashed bright. A warning.

Finnian's smile vanished.

Eldrin's hand went instinctively to the dagger as gold flared all around them. It burst through the air in a spiraling streak, scattering sparks like falling stars, and slammed into Eldrin's chest with a startled yelp and a poof of golden dust.

Eldrin reacted, swatting at the small creature on instinct. Silverwind snorted and danced sideways.

Finnian shouted, "WHAT IN ALL THE REALMS?"

Fizzlewing peeled himself off Eldrin's cloak, upside down, wings buzzing frantically as he flailed for balance. "I MADE IT!" he squeaked triumphantly, then immediately lost altitude and smacked into Eldrin again.

"Fizzlewing!" Eldrin cried.

The sprite froze mid-rant and turned around slowly. His eyes went wide. "You're not Silverwings," he breathed as his glow dimmed.

"It's good to see you too," Finnian said.

Fizzlewing swallowed hard and looked between them. "I am glad to see you..." he drawled, his gaze lingering on Finnian.

Finnian smiled, and the mark on his temples lit up.

Fizzlewing's smile faltered. He recoiled midair, wings buzzing wildly as gold motes spilled from him. "Oh my," he whispered, fluttering backward. "The second mark..."

Finnian huffed a breath, silver light spilling across his features. "Lucky me," he muttered.

Fizzlewing zipped around Finnian's head, his gold glow trailing behind. He flew close to the mark on each temple, hovering there, tilting his head as if listening to something only he could hear. The humor drained from his face. "No," Fizzlewing said quietly. "That's not luck."

Finnian frowned, reaching toward his temples.

Fizzlewing drifted back, just out of reach now. His wings slowed. His glow steadied, but did not brighten. "Well, then..." the sprite said a little too quickly, forcing a grin that didn't reach his eyes, "good thing I'm here!"

Finnian blinked and then looked at Eldrin, holding his gaze. A pause fell, heavy and waiting. Fizzlewing looked at Eldrin. Then at Finnian. And finally spoke.

"Because you're going to need me," he said. "Now, where..." He looked around. "Is Silverwings?"

The question landed harder than the roar ever could have. Eldrin's jaw tightened. Finnian opened his mouth, then thought better of it. Thalendir answered instead. "Gone."

Fizzlewing's wings stilled. "Gone?" he asked faintly.

"She returned to her kingdom," Eldrin said, glaring at Thalendir, forcing the words to sound steadier than they felt. "The drelves flew north."

Fizzlewing's glow dimmed another shade. "That's... not good."

The air tightened around them.

Eldrin's hand drifted slowly to the Aetherstone at his side. It was warm. Not burning. Not warning, but listening.

Thalendir's voice cut through the air. "If you're looking for her," he said coolly, "don't bother. She wouldn't recognize you anyway."

Eldrin glared at Thalendir, the tips of his ears reddening. "She sacrificed her memory of me for my life," he said, his voice rough. "To the Tree Sage."

Fizzlewing's wings stopped beating. Just for a breath. He dipped in the air, catching himself at the last moment, gold motes falling like spent sparks. When he steadied, his glow was dimmer than before. He did not look at Finnian or Thalendir. His eyes stayed on Eldrin. "Oh," he whispered. "Then you're going the wrong way."

"The wrong way?" Eldrin asked, turning to Fizzlewing.

The sprite did not answer. He zipped around Eldrin's head, wings fluttering like mad.

"We're going home," said Finnian. "How can that be the wrong way?"

"Wrong. Very wrong," Fizzlewing said, flying erratically, his tail sputtering a gold trail as he darted in front of Eldrin, blocking the path. "Home is where things stay," he said, wings buzzing hard. "Not where they change."

Eldrin's hand tightened around the reins. "You're not making sense."

"That's because you're not listening," Fizzlewing snapped. He gestured wildly at Eldrin's side. "Ask that."

Eldrin looked down. His hand closed around the Aetherstone. It didn't warm. It didn't glow. It did nothing at all.

"See?" Fizzlewing said.

Eldrin loosened his grip on the reins and turned Silverwind a fraction away from the descending trail. The Aetherstone stirred. Not heat. Not light. A faint pulse, like a breath finally released.

Fizzlewing crossed his front legs and raised a brow as he froze midair.

Eldrin swallowed. Silence folded around them.

"What are you doing?" Thalendir's voice cut through the stillness, sharp as frost.

Eldrin did not turn. "We're going this way," he said.

Thalendir laughed once, short and incredulous. "No. We're going home."

Eldrin's hand tightened on the reins. "The stone says otherwise."

Thalendir's eyes flicked to his side. "So you do everything the stone tells you to do?"

Fizzlewing hissed softly. Finnian shifted uneasily in his saddle.

"No, but it's time I did," Eldrin said. "If I had listened in the Arden, the dark elves would never have captured us."

"Father will expect both of us," Thalendir continued, voice smooth now. Dangerous. "And I will not tell him you wandered off chasing a feeling."

"Then don't."

Silence snapped tight between them. The vein on Thalendir's forehead pulsed. Eldrin's hand did not move from the stone at his side. The two brothers sat still on their mounts, eyeing one another.

Master Aldareth approached, one eyebrow raised. "What's going on?" Aldareth asked.

"Eldrin wants to go that way," Thalendir said lightly, nodding toward the fork in the trail.

Aldareth's gaze shifted to Eldrin. "Is that so?"

Eldrin didn't hesitate. "Yes," he said.

Thalendir scoffed softly.

"And why," Aldareth asked calmly, "would you turn away from home?"

Eldrin's fingers tightened once around the Aetherstone. It warmed at his touch. Fizzlewing landed on his shoulder, a shimmer of gold dust lighting his face. "Because home isn't the answer," Eldrin said.

Aldareth studied Eldrin's face. Then he glanced at the sprite on his shoulder and sat still for a long moment. "Answer to what?" he finally asked, looking at Eldrin.

Eldrin looked into the Master Trainer's eyes, then to his brother, and finally to Finnian. "To everything," he said.

Aldareth sat for several long moments, reins crossed, one hand resting on his saddle horn.

"And I suppose you'll be accompanying him?" Master Aldareth said as he lifted his chin toward Finnian.

"Aye," said Finnian with a sigh. He turned Embermane toward Eldrin and the lesser trail.

"And where is this path meant to lead?" Aldareth asked.

Fizzlewing lifted his chin, wings humming softly. "Somewhere that still remembers."

Aldareth studied him, then exhaled. "Aelar," he said.

The broad-shouldered elf straightened at once, and Aldareth found his gaze. "You'll go with them." A pause. "You answer to Prince Eldrin."

"Very well, sir," Aelar said, nodding to Master Aldareth. He reined his gelding onto the trail behind Eldrin, then waited.

Thalendir said nothing. His gaze lingered on Aelar, then Finnian, then finally on Eldrin. He turned Steel sharply beneath him and did not look back.

Chapter 6

High in the drelf realm, above the mist, where shadows stretched long across the cliffs, the Seer frowned. Her fingers drifted over the bone-and-crystal charms arranged before her, each one humming with a different strand of fate.

Something... shifted. A ripple through the land. A disturbance threaded beneath the breath of the world. Small to most, but to her, unmistakable. The balance had tipped.

She felt the power coil and unfurl like dawn reaching over distant peaks, seeking, choosing, binding. It touched the elf like a hesitant hand upon a forgotten door. The newly marked one. Chosen by prophecy. One who did not yet understand the shape of the burden laid upon him, nor the storm that would follow.

Nyxari's lashes lowered, her breath cooling the charms. But it wasn't the marked elf that concerned her. It was the glow beneath the charms. The faint, pulsing outline, etched not in light, but in fire. Its silhouette flickered across the spread of charms like a heartbeat struggling to surface, then vanished, leaving only the scent of smoke and the echo of distant wings.

Nyxari's fingers hovered above the embers of the vision. "A dragon," she whispered. "It can't be." But the charms trembled. And far below the cliffs, in the bones of the world, something answered with a low, rolling rumble, old as ruin, hungry as shadow.

By the time the reverberation faded from the bones of the world, the drelf kingdom was awake and moving. Lyria and Kaelis crossed the outer ridge of the walls together, glancing over the battlefield. The drelves had been busy, and the scars had already faded. Fallen stone had been cleared from the gates. The shattered watchtower now stood braced with fresh timber and iron bands. Smoke rose not from ruin, but from cook fires, steady and purposeful.

The dead were gone. Buried or burned, and remembered. Lyria felt it as a weight beneath her wings as she descended, the quiet labor of survival continuing without her permission. The drelf kingdom had not waited for her. Life moved on. It had to.

Nyxari waited for them near the inner gate, her dark braids stirring softly in the mountain wind. When Lyria and Kaelis landed, the Seer inclined her head, not in greeting, but in recognition. "You felt it," Nyxari said.

Lyria's brow furrowed. "Felt what?"

Nyxari's gaze lifted briefly toward the tall peaks beyond the city. "The cry," she said.

Kaelis stiffened.

Lyria's wings twitched once. "A dragon?"

Nyxari did not answer immediately. "Very good," she said at last. "Your perception grows."

Lyria nodded. "The mark burned. Like anger."

Nyxari's eyes returned to hers. "Darkness does not always wake angry," she breathed. "Sometimes it wakes hungry."

Lyria flexed her wings and met Nyxari's gaze. "Isn't that the same thing?"

Nyxari's mouth curved faintly. "No," she said. "Anger burns. Hunger endures."

The words settled between them, heavy as ash.

Kaelis broke the silence. "And the council?" she asked, one eyebrow raised. "Do they know of it?"

"They know of the second mark choosing the elf," Nyxari said. "And of your victory in freeing the captives." She studied them both for a long moment, measuring, weighing. "You should rest," she said.

Lyria exhaled slowly. Her wings ached; her bones still carried the echo of fire and stone. "And then?"

Nyxari's gaze sharpened. "Then we decide what the council should know."

Chapter 7

The Abyss did not echo. It *listened.*

Vartharax felt the sound before it reached him, not through ears, but through the chains wound around his essence, the ancient Covenant magic biting deep into scale and bone and something far older. For a long moment, the great dragon did nothing. No roar. No struggle. Only a slow, deliberate inhale that drew heat from the shadows themselves.

He felt it again. Faint. Far away. But there. Beyond the bounds of the Abyss, something had shifted, a ripple in the weave of life and death. A presence the darkness recognized.

His massive form shifted within the Abyss, chains groaning, not breaking, but adjusting, as if his awareness unsettled the magic itself. From the deepest recesses of his twisted soul, a thought formed.

If light could tip the scales, so could shadow.

A slit of molten gold cut through the dark as he opened one eye. His lips curled into a slow, terrible smile. The chamber stilled around him. "There is a way," he murmured. "If the balance breaks toward the dark, my chains break."

The chains tightened in answer. Vartharax smiled anyway.

The mark-bearers had stirred the prophecy. And prophecy... had stirred something else. Something that could tip the scales again.

There was one who had served him before. One scarred by failure. One desperate enough to answer. But to reach him, Vartharax would have to call him back from death, or something far more cruel.

The pulse came again. This time it was sharper, commanding. Drakor bared his fangs, not in submission, but in pain and recognition.

So. You still breathe.

The cavern shuddered, dust cascading from the ceiling as the darkness pressed inward. The call deepened, no longer probing. Now a summons. A command.

Drakor forced himself upright, every shattered bone screaming in protest. A jagged smile split his battered face. "You need me," he whispered.

The earth trembled again, answering him with the weight of the dark lord's will. "I hear you," Drakor growled at last, the words tasting like ash. "I always do."

His eyes burned as he lifted his head toward the dark beyond the cave. But this time... he smiled wider. This time, he would answer on his own terms. For now, he would let Vartharax believe the old order still held.

Let him believe obedience still meant loyalty.

Chapter 8

Finnian had always thought of himself as adaptable. Fast on his feet. Quick with a grin. The sort who could roll with whatever the world threw at him. But the mark unsettled him. Its presence. The pressure. Like a hand resting too long on his thoughts.

Lyria was right about the mark. It changed everything.

Eldrin rode ahead, quiet in a way Finnian recognized. Not doubt, or fear, but purpose. Fizzlewing hovered near his shoulder, wings barely moving. For once, he did not fidget. He simply followed.

Behind them, the forest shifted. Not dramatically. Not enough for anyone else to comment on. But Finnian felt it. The mark was listening. Anticipating. The pressure behind his eyes tightened as Eldrin slowed ahead, Silverwind's ears pricked, his posture subtly shifting.

"Left," Finnian said suddenly. The words landed before Eldrin could speak.

Eldrin closed his mouth and stared at him.

"Just a feeling," Finnian said, shrugging. He didn't like knowing things before they happened. Apparently, the mark didn't mind.

Eldrin said nothing, but he studied Finnian's face, not searching for humor, not waiting for the rest of the joke. This time, he looked deeper, as if trying to see beneath the surface. He turned Silverwind's head to the left, and the Aetherstone at his side pulsed once, faint and steady.

Aelar watched from a few paces back, his expression unreadable. His gaze flicked from Finnian to Eldrin, to the stone, then to the narrowing trail ahead. When Eldrin urged his horse forward, Aelar followed without hesitation.

The group settled into a quiet rhythm, the steady cadence of hooves drawing them into the same slow breath. Somewhere between one step and the next, Eldrin hummed, soft and unthinking. A thread of sound he hadn't realized he remembered.

It wasn't a tune so much as a shape, familiar in the way of things learned before words. He was soon lost in the melody, unaware that fragments long forgotten were taking shape.

The trail wove on as thickets closed around them. Weariness settled into their bones, stealing the need for sound.

Finnian was the first to break the silence. "I don't know where this path leads," he said, shifting in the saddle, "but if it doesn't involve food soon, I'm going to lose my last shred of goodwill toward destiny."

Eldrin huffed a quiet breath almost a laugh. "And while you're scheming up some food, why not add a cup of Gantar's finest?"

Finnian grinned. "Now you're speaking my language."

"And a soft bed," said Fizzlewing as he buzzed around them.

Both elves glanced at the sprite, suddenly considering the idea.

"As long as we're dreaming..." he said.

They settled back into a steady cadence, the sound of hooves on dirt filling the space where words had been. Each caught up in their own daydreams.

Ahead, the trail curved, widening as the trees thinned. A light flickered. Not torchlight. Hearthlight. A low cluster of buildings emerged from the dusk, stone and timber, warm smoke rising steadily into the cooling air.

A waystation.

Finnian sagged in his saddle. "Oh, bless whatever ancient power put that there."

Fizzlewing hovered forward, wings slowing. "Told you. Never hurts to dream."

As they approached, fatigue finally caught up with them. A young elf stepped out from beside the nearest stable, brushing his hands on his trousers. He couldn't have been much older than Finnian, dark hair pulled back, eyes bright with the quiet curiosity of someone used to travelers passing through.

"Evening," he said easily. "I can take your horses, if you'd like. There's water and feed already laid out."

Finnian didn't hesitate. He slid from the saddle with a grateful groan. "You're a miracle."

The elf smiled, taking their reins. "If you're staying the night, the common room's warm. Bartender can sort you out, food, rooms, whatever you need."

Eldrin nodded his thanks, and for the first time since leaving the trail, the tightness in his shoulders eased.

As they stepped inside, warmth wrapped around them, heavy with the scent of woodsmoke and ale. Their eyes took a moment to adjust, firelight glinting off sturdy wooden tables and scarred floors worn smooth by countless travelers.

Eldrin led the way to an empty table away from the door. Finnian pulled his cloak a little higher as they crossed the threshold, choosing a seat out of the firelight, while Fizzlewing slipped upward, settling among the rafters where the shadows clung. Aelar settled into a chair beside Finnian, grateful for warmth and the promise of a full belly.

Inside, the common room hummed with quiet conversation. And in the corner, half-hidden by shadow and firelight, a figure sat alone with an untouched cup, listening. A dark cloak covered his head, but the weathered hands resting on the table spoke of many moons seen wax and wane.

Eldrin's fingers stilled against the table. At his side, the Aetherstone warmed, just barely. Finnian shifted in his chair. The silver lines at his temples prickled, a faint pressure blooming and then easing, like a breath held too long and finally released. He frowned, tugging his cloak forward without thinking.

Aelar noticed the movement. His gaze flicked from Finnian to Eldrin, then lingered, watchful, unreadable. Whatever this place was, it was not empty.

A shadow shifted near the bar and headed their way. The bartender was a gruff fellow, white beard, pointed ears, and a voice that sounded like smoke and stories had worn it smooth. He wiped his hands on his apron as he approached. "Evening," he said, rough but not unkind. "You look like you've ridden hard. Stew's on, ale's fresh, and there's beds upstairs if you're staying."

"We'll take one of each, thank you," said Finnian, a little too eager as he tossed a few coins onto the table.

Eldrin inclined his head, the barest hint of a smile touching his mouth before it was gone.

"Stew and ale all around, then," the bartender said, already turning away. "You can pay for the beds before going up."

The scrape of a chair and the crackle of the hearth filled the space he left behind. Warmth lingered in the room as the fire crackled on. Voices murmured as before. Someone laughed near the bar. A spoon clinked against a bowl.

And yet, cold brushed the back of Finnian's neck.

It wasn't a draft. But something else.

His gaze drifted unbidden to the cloaked figure in the corner. To the untouched cup before the stranger. It hadn't steamed or cooled. It had simply... waited. As though time had forgotten it.

Finnian swallowed. The silver at his temples tightened, a quiet pressure blooming beneath his skin. Not sharp, not urgent, just present. Aware.

Aelar shifted, fingers brushing the hilt of his blade. He didn't draw it. Not yet. His eyes had already narrowed, tracking the room with the calm of someone who trusted his instincts more than his sight. Eldrin's hand went to the Aetherstone again. It felt strange beneath his fingers, as though it recognized something.

The cloaked figure in the corner did not move. Did not drink, or look their way. And still, the space around him felt occupied in a way the rest of the room did not.

Finnian exhaled slowly, careful not to draw attention to himself or the marks on his temples.

"The mark always notices first," the cloaked figure said softly, without looking up.

Eldrin's head turned. The voice was unmistakable, rooted in memories older than the road beneath his boots. "Gantar..." Eldrin said, exhaling.

The cloaked figure did not look up.

Finnian's brows knit. He glanced from Eldrin to the sage and said, "You've been expecting us."

Then, slowly, his gaze lifted to the rafters where Fizzlewing hovered, very still. Too still. "You knew," Finnian said quietly. It wasn't an accusation. It was a realization.

Fizzlewing winced. "Knew is a strong word."

Aelar straightened in his chair, hand resting casually near his blade, eyes never leaving the door. "Master Gantar doesn't appear without reason," he said at last.

Intense green eyes shone from beneath the cloak. "You're being followed," said the sage.

The dagger at Eldrin's side glowed blue as the door creaked open.

A burst of icy wind tore through the common room, snuffing candles and sending embers skittering across the hearth. The fire guttered, flames bowing low as if pressed by an unseen hand. Cloaks snapped. Cups rattled. Somewhere near the bar, someone swore under their breath.

Then the door slammed shut.

Chapter 9

Everyone in the common room jumped. Except Gantar. The silence that followed pressed heavy, as if the air itself waited for permission to move again. All eyes were on the door. Waiting. Expectant.

Until Gantar lifted his cup and drained it.

The room exhaled. Mugs clinked. Chairs scraped. Someone laughed a little too loudly, and conversation rushed back in as if it had never stopped at all.

Gantar stood and moved toward the three elves.

"Does this mean we don't get to eat?" Finnian asked, glancing toward the bar, eyes on the food headed their way.

The sage chuckled, soft and genuine, and rested a hand briefly between Finnian's shoulders. "Good to see you haven't changed."

Finnian grinned. "Some of us cling to our strengths."

Gantar's smile lingered a heartbeat longer than expected before his gaze lifted to Eldrin. The warmth faded, not into severity, but focus. "I'm not here to rob you of a well-deserved meal," he said. "You'll want food in your bellies before morning."

Eldrin inclined his head toward the empty chair at the table. "Welcome, Gantar. Join us," he said. It wasn't a question.

Gantar studied him for a moment, something unreadable passing behind his eyes. Then he nodded once and took the seat, folding his hands on top of the table. "You chose the right road," the sage said quietly. "Even if you didn't yet know why."

Eldrin held his gaze. "I was hoping you'd tell me."

A corner of Gantar's mouth twitched. "In time."

Before Eldrin could press further, the bartender returned, arms laden with steaming bowls. He set them down with a practiced thump, thick stew, rich with herbs and root vegetables, the kind meant to stave off the cold and settle weary bones.

The scent alone made Finnian sigh. "Now this," he said, reaching for a spoon, "is what destiny should smell like."

Fizzlewing drifted lower, hovering just above the table, peering into a bowl with open approval.

"Eat," Gantar said again, softer this time. "Questions can wait. Hunger cannot."

For a moment, they did just that, spoons scraping, steam rising, the warmth of the meal easing the road from their shoulders. Outside, the wind brushed the shutters. Inside, the night waited.

The bartender returned a moment later with heavy mugs of ale, foam sloshing over the rims as he set them down. Finnian reached for one at once.

Gantar's hand stilled the mug with a gentle tap. Not a command, just enough. "Drink," the sage said, voice low. "But not too freely. You'll want a clear head when the road calls you again."

Finnian grimaced theatrically. "You really know how to ruin a good evening."

Gantar's eyes softened, though his tone did not. "I know how to keep you alive."

Finnian considered that, then nodded and took a measured sip. "Fair enough."

Eldrin lifted his mug but didn't drink yet. He met Gantar's gaze over the rim, understanding passing between them without words. Whatever lay ahead would not forgive dull senses.

When the last bowl was clean and the mugs sat empty between them, Eldrin leaned closer to Gantar, lowering his voice. "I assume," he said quietly, "that eventually you're going to tell me why you're here."

Gantar regarded him for a long moment, eyes steady in the firelight. "I am," he said at last. He rose from the table, cloak settling around him like a closing curtain. "But not here."

Outside, the wind whispered along the eaves. And somewhere beyond the walls, something listened.

They took the narrow stairs at the back of the common room, boots thudding softly on worn wood. The sounds of the tavern dulled behind them, replaced by the creak of beams and the low hush of wind pressing against the walls.

Their room was simple, three narrow beds pushed against opposite walls, a small washstand, and a single shuttered window that rattled faintly in the night breeze. A hearth sat cold in the corner, long unused. It was enough.

Boots were tugged off and dropped where they fell. Aelar stretched out on a bed at once, rolling his shoulders as if only now allowing himself to feel the road. Finnian claimed another, sprawling back with a groan of relief. "Best mattress I've met all day," he declared.

Fizzlewing drifted in lazy circles near the ceiling, inspecting the rafters with exaggerated care before settling atop a beam, wings folded tight. Eldrin remained standing a moment longer, listening to the building, to the night beyond it, and to the absence of answers.

Gantar closed the door quietly behind them. "We'll stay just long enough for you to get some sleep," he said at last. "But keep your weapons close and your belts cinched."

Finnian cracked one eye open. "That's comforting."

"It's the best I can do," Gantar replied, unoffended.

Eldrin turned to him. "So, what, or who, is following us?"

Gantar met his gaze. "I'm not entirely sure. But I have a hunch. And if I'm right, they will not risk revealing themselves yet."

A pause.

"Yet," Aelar echoed softly.

Gantar inclined his head. Outside, something moved along the edge of the night. Not close enough to touch. Not far enough to forget. "I'll keep watch," Gantar said. Then, without looking up, added, "With help."

Fizzlewing stiffened mid-hover. "Oh, no."

"You're better at sensing intent than any ward I could lay," Gantar said mildly.

"That's not a compliment," Fizzlewing muttered, but he drifted toward the door all the same.

Eldrin let out a slow breath. He was too exhausted to argue or press for more details. "Wake us if anything changes."

Gantar's eyes flicked to the window. To the dark beyond. "You'll be the first to know," he said.

One by one, they lay back. The beds creaked. The room settled, wood sighing softly as the building cooled. Sleep came slowly, thin and watchful.

And outside, the night waited.

Eldrin slept.

Or thought he did.

The room faded, not into darkness, but into silver light, thin as mist and warm as breath. The smell of hearth smoke gave way to something older. Resin. Snowmelt. Song. A familiar voice hummed. Low and gentle.

Eldrin stood barefoot on smooth stone, the world around him vast and hollow, like the inside of a mountain carved by time. Light spilled down from above in slow, drifting shafts, catching motes of dust that shimmered like stars.

Before him, a female elf knelt. Silver hair fell loose down her back, threaded with pale gold. Her hands rested on the hilt of a dagger planted point-down in the stone.

“Mother,” Eldrin breathed.

She did not turn. But the humming changed, shifted, layering over itself. Not one voice now, but many, braided together. Elven. Draconic. Something else beneath it, deeper and aching. A song without words. The one he had hummed earlier.

The dagger glowed blue, then gold, twined, flowing together like breath and flame learning how to share the same space.

The stone beneath Eldrin's feet thrummed in answer. From the far edge of the light, a figure appeared. A young she-elf, golden hair catching the glow, eyes the same green as Thariel's. She stood apart, watching as if she had always been there, just beyond his sight. There was sorrow in her stillness. And resolve.

Eldrin's chest tightened. "Who are you?" he asked.

The elf lifted her gaze. Her lips parted, and the song broke. His dagger rang out once, sharp and clear.

Eldrin gasped and jerked upright.

Gantar's hand closed around his wrist. "Now," his voice snapped with urgency. "Eldrin. We must go."

The room was dark and cold. Eldrin swung his legs over the side of the bed, heart still racing from silver light and song and a face he could not place.

Finnian was already awake. So was Aelar. But something was wrong. Eldrin's gaze flicked to the door. Then the rafters. Then the window.

"Where's Fizzlewing?" Finnian asked. The words landed harder than they should have.

Gantar did not answer at once. Outside, the wind scraped softly along the shutters, slow and deliberate, as though listening.

"I sent him ahead," the old sage said at last.

Eldrin stilled. "Ahead... where?"

Gantar met his gaze without flinching. "To the one who needs him more than we do right now."

Eldrin's breath caught. "Lyria."

Gantar inclined his head. "The song you carry," he said quietly, "was never meant for you alone."

Eldrin stared at him. "How do you know about the song?"

Gantar's expression did not change, but something old stirred behind his eyes. "Because songs like that do not wake without consequence," he said. "And they do not choose only one heart."

Finnian swallowed. His hand rose, unthinking, to his temples. "She felt it," he said. Not a question.

"Yes," Gantar replied. "And she will not understand why."

Hope flared, sharp and dangerous, in Eldrin's chest. "Will it help her remember me?" he asked.

Gantar's voice softened, but only just. "It will help her remember something," he said. "That is how it begins."

Outside, something moved. Not close enough to see, but close enough to feel.

The Aetherstone burned against Eldrin's side as the group gathered their gear and hurried down the stairs. The cold was waiting for them.

The stable crouched behind the waystation like a held breath. Lantern light spilled in thin, wavering bands across packed earth and rough-hewn beams. Horses shifted in their stalls, leather creaked softly, and the air smelled of hay, sweat, and cold iron.

Eldrin moved quickly, cloak pulled close, one hand already reaching for Silverwind's reins. Gantar had readied their horses, thankfully.

"Quiet," Aelar murmured.

He had stopped walking. The others hadn't noticed the shift. His gaze tracked the center aisle. One horse there, not theirs, had lifted its head, ears pinned forward, nostrils flaring as if catching a scent it didn't like. Aelar's hand drifted closer to his blade.

Finnian felt it a heartbeat later. Pressure. The mark on his temples tightened, awareness blooming sharp and cold beneath his skin. He opened his mouth to speak as Eldrin stepped forward and ran solidly into someone. Not a shadow. Not empty air. A body.

Broad shoulders. Familiar weight. The soft exhale of breath just inches from his own. Eldrin staggered back half a step, fingers instinctively reaching for his dagger.

"Careful." The voice was calm. Too calm.

Eldrin froze. He knew that voice.

Lantern light caught the edge of a face, golden hair, eyes steady and unreadable, armor dark beneath a travel cloak.

"Thalendir?" Eldrin breathed.

The name settled heavily between them. Horses stamped. A chain clinked softly somewhere in the dark.

Thalendir's gaze flicked briefly over Eldrin's shoulder, taking in Finnian and Aelar. Then it stopped on Gantar.

The sage stood a few paces back, face half-shadowed by the lantern's swing. Their eyes met as understanding passed between them, quiet, complete. Gantar did not speak.

"So," Thalendir said at last, breaking the silence as he addressed Eldrin. "Sneaking out before dawn again?"

Eldrin swallowed. "I thought..."

"Well, you thought wrong," Thalendir said.

For the first time, Gantar moved. Just one step. Not forward, aside, into the lantern's reach. Enough to place himself fully in the lantern light. His silence spoke loudly.

Loud enough for the others to realize this moment was not accidental.

Finnian shifted, glancing between them. "Should I be offended that no one told me we were collecting brothers along the way?"

No one laughed.

Thalendir's gaze returned to Eldrin. "I couldn't let you have all the fun. Brother," he said.

Another silence. Thicker now. Outside the stable, wind whispered against wood and stone. Somewhere beyond the waystation, something listened.

Chapter 10

King Eldermyst stood alone, wringing his hands. It had been days since he'd received word of his sons. And now, Gantar was gone.

The council chamber lay empty behind him, its long table cleared, its banners hanging still. Dawn crept pale and unwelcome through the top windows, catching on the silver threads in his hair and the deep lines carved by worry across his brow.

Gantar did not vanish without a purpose. That knowledge did little to ease the tightness in his chest. Footsteps echoed beyond the doors—measured, familiar.

"Enter," Eldermyst said, straightening at once, his hands falling still at his sides.

The doors opened, and Master Aldareth stepped inside. His armor bore the dust of hard riding, his expression carefully neutral, though the strain beneath it was unmistakable.

"You returned sooner than expected," the king said.

"A necessity, my lord," Aldareth replied, bowing. "I brought back those you ordered to aid the drelves. They are battle-weary and in need of rest. The drelf defenses are holding. The wounded are tended."

Eldermyst nodded. Those were the answers of a man who followed orders. "And my sons?" the king asked quietly.

Aldareth did not answer at once. "Prince Eldrin did not return," Aldareth said. "He had chosen a different road, one the prophecy favors. But Prince Thalendir was with us. Is he not here?"

The words settled like frost.

Eldermyst turned toward the window, jaw tightening. Beyond the glass, the forest stirred in the early light, peaceful, indifferent.

"He is not. And neither is Gantar," the king said.

Aldareth's gaze lifted. "Thalendir must have changed his mind," he said. "And gone after Eldrin."

"That doesn't sound like Thalendir," Eldermyst said. "Unless... Gantar had something to do with convincing him." His breath left him slowly. "Do you know where they went?"

"Only that when the road forked above Larimar Falls, they went their own way," Aldareth said, lowering his head. "Forgive me, Lord, but Eldrin was not to be swayed from his path."

The king's eyes closed for a heartbeat. "And now they are all gone again," the king whispered. He clenched his fists and raised one to his mouth.

Aldareth hesitated, then spoke carefully. "With respect, my king... I'm certain Gantar must be with them. He has always known when to move unseen."

"I told him to gather those loyal to me," Eldermyst said. "I did not tell him to vanish. Or put my sons in more danger."

Silence stretched between them.

At last, Eldermyst turned back, resolve hardening where worry had been. "I assume Finnian stayed with Eldrin?" he asked.

"Yes, he remained with Prince Eldrin," Aldareth said. "And I sent Aelar as well."

That, at least, was something.

Eldermyst nodded once. "Then Eldrin is not alone."

"No," Aldareth agreed.

The king's lips pressed into a thin line.

"I can take some of my best warriors and go after them," Master Aldareth said, lowering himself onto one knee.

Eldermyst did not answer at once. He looked down at Aldareth, at the kneeling Master Trainer who had shaped generations of elven warriors, who had never once failed him in battle or counsel. "No," the king said at last.

Aldareth lifted his head, surprise flickering across his features before he masked it.

"They chose this path," Eldermyst continued. "If I send an armed force after them now, the council will know. And if the council knows, so will our enemies."

He turned away, pacing once before the tall windows, hands clasped behind his back. "Gantar believed secrecy was our shield," he said. "I will not tear it away out of fear."

Aldareth bowed his head. "Then what would you have me do, my king?"

Eldermyst stopped. When he spoke again, his voice was steady, but the weight in it was unmistakable. "Remain here," he said. "Watch the council. Listen more than you speak. And if word comes, any word, of my sons or Gantar..."

Aldareth's jaw set. "You will have it at once."

Eldermyst nodded. "Good," he said. "Because whatever road they've taken, I suspect it will not remain hidden for long."

The wind rose outside, rattling the tall windows. King Eldermyst stared out at the forest, toward paths he could not see. "I need you to help finish what Gantar started," the king said at last. "Find those we can still trust. And bring me their names."

"As you wish, my lord," Aldareth said.

"Go now," the king said.

Aldareth rose and bowed his head. Just before he withdrew, the king spoke again.

"Thank you, Master Aldareth," Eldermyst said quietly. "For your loyal service."

Aldareth paused.

"My sons are no longer elflings," the king continued. "They are warriors. Heirs. Princes." His voice did not waver, but something unspoken passed beneath it. "Not even I can stop them from fulfilling their destiny."

Aldareth bowed his head, clicked his heels, and exited the room.

Eldermyst remained where he was, alone once more in the vast chamber.

Find those we can still trust.

Gantar's warning echoed in his thoughts. And for the first time since ascending the throne, the king wondered whether the greatest threat to his realm would come from beyond its borders, or from within them.

And somewhere beyond the reach of crown and council, his sons walked paths he could no longer see.

Chapter 11

Another tremor rolled through the stone, subtle, impatient. Drakor felt it and smiled. He stepped fully into the open, moonlight catching the torn edges of his wings, the scars that were not yet healed. He lifted his head and tasted the air.

Marks were stirring and old magic was waking. A song moving through the world again, bringing change.

"So," he murmured, voice rough with amusement. "The board is being reset."

The pull from the Abyss came again, distant, demanding. Drakor did not answer. If the balance could be tipped, then it could be steered. And he had no intention of kneeling to a master again.

"You want the dark to rise," he said softly, imagining the ancient presence straining against its chains. "Very well."

His claws bit into the stone as he spread his wings. "But this time," Drakor added, a jagged smile cutting across his ruined face, "it will answer to me."

He launched into the night, not toward the call, but toward the places where fear already waited to be gathered. Let Vartharax wait.

Drakor had work to do.

He flew to where he knew they would be. Not to ruins. Not to battlefields picked clean by scavengers and crows. But to the places survivors always gathered, where shadows pooled, where anger fermented, and plans were whispered instead of shouted.

The night swallowed him as he crossed the ridgelines, wings cutting the air in long, punishing strokes. Each beat sent fire through torn muscle and bruised bone, but Drakor welcomed it. Pain meant progress.

Below him, the land changed. Forests thinned. Stone broke through soil in jagged spines. Old roads, abandoned and half-swallowed by roots, threaded the dark like scars that never healed properly.

He circled once, high and silent. Then he felt it. A bitterness that clung to the land itself, resentment soaked deep into earth, bark, and bone. The aftermath of defeat, sharpened into something colder than grief.

Drakor descended. He landed beyond the firelight, wings folding with a hiss of displaced air. From the treeline, he watched them gather, cloaked figures moving with purpose, weapons stacked, voices low and urgent.

Survivors. Hunters licking their wounds. Dark elves.

Drakor's lip curled. Good. They had lost. They were angry and afraid.

He stepped forward, and a branch snapped. Steel hissed free of sheaths as shadows shifted. Someone gasped when they saw him.

Drakor let the silence stretch, just long enough for recognition to dawn, for terror to ripple outward like a dropped stone in black water. "I know why you're here," he said, his voice carrying without effort, threading through the trees and into their chests.

No one spoke.

"I know what you lost," he continued. "And who you blame."

A pause. "I know the song you heard, and why it frightened you."

That did it. Murmurs broke the stillness. Heads turned. A hand tightened on a spear.

Drakor's eyes gleamed. "You seek power," he hissed. "So do I." He lowered his head just slightly, not in submission, but invitation.

"Walk with me," Drakor murmured. "I will show you where the balance breaks."

A beat. "And how to take back what belongs to you."

Far beyond sight, the pulse shuddered as Vartharax waited. Drakor smiled.

"Why should we trust you?" came the voice from the shadows. "You want the power of the marks for yourself. And you've already failed, several times."

A murmur rippled through the clearing. Steel shifted. Fingers tightened around spear shafts and curved blades.

From the darkness stepped Drovane, ruler of the dark elves. Tall. Spare. Cloaked in black leather etched with sigils that drank the firelight instead of reflecting it. His eyes were pale, too pale, set in a face carved by patience rather than rage.

Drakor did not bristle. He laughed, a sound like stone grinding against bone. "You mistake failure for finality," Drakor said. "That is why you hide in forests and ruins... while he rots in chains."

The word, *he,* needed no name.

Drovane's gaze sharpened. "Careful."

"We all failed," Drakor continued, lifting his head. His broken wings twitched, not weak, restrained. "Because they outsmarted us." He stepped closer to the fire, close enough that heat kissed his scales.

"But they are scattered. Divided. Weak," said Drakor.

A dangerous silence followed.

Drovane studied him. "And what does he say?"

Drakor's smile widened. "He is bound," he said. "And needs us this time."

He lowered his head again, just enough to seem deferential. "You want the marks," Drakor went on. "You want the song silenced, and you want the lie burned away so your kind can rise again."

A pause.

"I want the same end," he said. "And... I am the one Vartharax calls."

The fire cracked loudly. Somewhere in the ranks, someone shifted, uncertain now.

Drovane did not move. "And when you decide we are no longer useful?" he asked.

Drakor met his eyes, unblinking. "Then you will already have power enough that I cannot discard you," he said.

The fire popped, sending a spiral of sparks into the night. Shadows leapt across the faces of the gathered Umbrin, some hard with hunger, others tight with caution.

Drovane tilted his head a fraction. "You speak as though the future is decided."

Drakor's claws scraped stone as he shifted his weight. "No," he said. "I speak as though it is moving."

He lifted his gaze, not to the dark elves, but beyond them. Toward the mountains. Toward the unseen roads where fate was bending. "The powers have awakened," Drakor continued. "Not all who play their part understand what they carry, yet."

A ripple passed through the clearing. Drovane's eyes narrowed. "You claim much."

"I claim timing," Drakor replied. "And I claim this: if you move before Vartharax can free himself, the song will bind him forever."

He leaned forward, lowering his voice. "But if you wait, while the marks lie scattered, while the song stays unfinished..."

He straightened. "He will return."

Silence.

Then Drovane stepped closer to the fire, its light carving sharp planes along his face. "And what would you have us do?" he asked.

Drakor's smile returned. His wings flexed once, casting a long shadow across the stones. "Follow me," Drakor said softly. "And we will take the marks, then decide what the world owes us."

The elves stood silent, waiting for their leader to speak. And in the Abyss, far from fire and forest, Vartharax waited too.

Drakor's gaze lifted, unfocused now, as though his thoughts had moved far beyond the clearing. "The elf with the fire in his soul does not yet know what he carries," he rasped. "Or what power it yields."

Drovane stared at the dragon before him, eyes narrowed, not in fear, but calculation.

"And you know where to find him?"

"I know the road he took," Drakor said. "And where it leads."

The fire cracked.

"You speak with confidence," Drovane said. "For one who crawls back to us broken."

Drakor's jaw tightened, but he did not rise to the bait. "I crawled back alive."

A pause.

Drovane nodded once, as if conceding a minor point.

Drakor's eyes gleamed. "Then you will help me?" he said.

Drovane's gaze drifted, not to Drakor, but to a figure standing at the edge of the clearing. A scout. Mud on his boots. Breath still uneven. Drakor felt it then. Movement that was not his.

Drovane spoke without turning. "Our eyes are already on the road," he said calmly.

The words landed like a blade between Drakor's scales. "You move quickly," Drakor said.

"We learned to," Drovane replied. "Waiting is what nearly ended us."

A pause.

"They left before dusk," Drovane continued. "Careful trackers. They will not engage. Not yet."

Drakor inclined his head, slow and deliberate, forcing his fury down into silence. "Wise," he said.

Drovane finally turned to him. "If the elf is where we believe he is," he said, "my troops will already be there."

Drakor nodded. "Very well." But his wings twitched once.

Drovane stepped closer, firelight reflecting in Drakor's battered scales. "Perhaps we can work together," he added softly, "if you wish to keep pace."

Drakor met his gaze. "I never fall behind."

Drovane inclined his head. "Then you'll have no trouble catching up."

He stepped back into shadow. Dark figures shifted through the trees behind him, silent and watchful.

Drovane pulled his hood tighter, the smile never quite leaving his mouth.

Let the dragon fail again.

Chapter 12

Lyria woke with a sharp inhale. Her heart raced.

The room was dark, the drelf kingdom quiet beyond the walls, but something gold glimmered near the window. Hovering.

She pushed herself upright. "Hello...?"

The small glowing sprite tilted in the air, wings buzzing unevenly. "Oh," he breathed. "You're awake."

Relief loosened her chest. "Fizzlewing?"

His glow brightened. "Silverwings. I'm here to help."

"With what?"

"To help you remember."

Lyria's hand rose to her neck. "You mean the elf?" She shook her head. "I don't remember him."

Fizzlewing dimmed slightly. "But you knew the voice. The one from your dream."

"Yes," she whispered. "How did you know?"

"Connections," he said gently.

"It aches," Lyria said, her hand sliding to her chest. "But I can't remember why."

Fizzlewing settled on her shoulder. "The heart never forgets. Even when the mind wants to."

Outside the door, boots stopped short on stone. Kaelis stilled, hand drifting to her blade. Voices, low and strained, came from inside. She leaned closer, pressing her ear to the wood as a thin line of gold light slipped beneath the crack between floor and door.

The corner of Kaelis's mouth turned upward. *Fizzlewing.* She rapped her knuckles lightly against the door.

"Lyria," she said.

The sound startled Lyria. Her hand dropped from her chest at once, fingers curling into the blanket as she pulled the covers higher, shielding herself by instinct. As if Kaelis might see straight through skin and bone, into the ache she couldn't name.

Kaelis's hand settled on the knob, fingers tracing grooves worn smooth by time. She had turned it a thousand times before, when sleep wouldn't come, when grief pressed too close, when the world felt too heavy to face alone.

She slipped inside, closing the door behind her with the same care she'd used all those years ago. Her gaze swept the room in a single, practiced glance, window, shadows, the small golden sprite hovering near the bed, before settling on Lyria.

“I heard him too,” Kaelis said.

Her gaze flicked at once to the blanket drawn tight across Lyria’s chest, an old, familiar shield meant to guard what Kaelis already knew. She crossed the room and sat on the edge of the bed, close, but not crowding.

Lyria swallowed and let out a breath that almost passed for steady.

“He’s been busy,” Kaelis said, her gaze settling on Fizzlewing.

The sprite puffed up at once, wings flaring indignantly. “Hello?” he said. “I’m right here, you know.”

Neither of them looked at him.

His glow wavered. “...Also,” he added, crossing his front legs, “for the record, I was invited here.”

Kaelis’s mouth twitched. “Really?”

Fizzlewing slowed his wings.

Lyria let out a quiet breath, the realization settling slowly. The song had reached another.

Nyxari had been waiting for the echo to return. It came sooner than she expected. Not as sound or fire, but as a tightening, subtle and insistent, beneath the threads she held between her fingers. She stilled as the bone-and-crystal charms before her trembled. Not all of them. Only the oldest. The ones she had never fully trusted.

The echo moved, and Nyxari's eyes opened. It was not rising from the Abyss. Nor did it burn with the fury she had learned to fear. This was different. It was hungrier. Patient.

She followed the pull, not downward, but sideways. Along forgotten paths. Along memory and song. "So," she murmured. "It stirs."

The threads crossed between marked and unmarked. Between light and shadow. And dragon.

Nyxari exhaled slowly. Far below, within stone walls and guarded hearts, Lyria ached for something she could not name. And far beyond her sight, something vast and ancient lifted its head.

Nyxari closed her hand around the charms.

So it begins.

Chapter 13

They did not leave the waystation by the road. Eldrin led them through the back paddock and into the treeline beyond, where the ground dipped and the frost clung longer to the roots. Dawn was still a pale rumor behind the hills, the uneasy hour when night had not yet decided whether to release its hold.

A fine rain was falling. Not enough to soak. Just enough to whisper.

Silverwind flicked her ears, uneasy. Embermane snorted once, then stilled and stepped lighter than usual. Eldrin felt it then, unease. Even the wind held its breath.

Behind him, Finnian shifted in his saddle. "Tell me I'm imagining things," he murmured.

Gantar answered before Eldrin could. "You are not," the sage said quietly. Rain darkened his cloak, beading along the folds, but he did not look to the sky. His gaze remained fixed ahead, unfocused, listening in a way that had nothing to do with sound.

Eldrin raised a fist, and the others stopped. Aelar slid from his horse without a word, crouching near the disturbed earth at the edge of the trees. His fingers brushed the soil once, then again, lighter this time. "Tracks," he breathed. "Careful ones."

"How careful?" Finnian asked.

Aelar's jaw tightened. "Enough to want us to miss them."

That was when the mark flared, without warning. Finnian gasped, clutching the side of his head as silver light streaked briefly across his temples, too bright, too fast. Not direction. Noise, movement without shape, intent without form, flooded his senses. He staggered, grabbing Embermane's saddle to steady himself.

"Finn," Eldrin said sharply.

"I'm..." Finnian swallowed hard. "I'm fine. I just..."

The pressure spiked again. Closer this time. "No," he blurted. "I don't think they're behind us."

Thalendir reined in beside him. "You're guessing."

Finnian shook his head, breath shallow. "No. I'm... listening."

The word tasted strange in his mouth.

Gantar's fingers tightened around his staff. "Yes," the sage said softly. "That is what unsettles you."

The rain thickened. Not heavier, colder.

Eldrin felt the Aetherstone warm, not hot, not urgent, but taut, like a drawn string waiting to be loosed.

Ahead, a branch creaked. Aelar rose slowly, blade half-drawn.

Thalendir's gaze swept the treeline, his usual sharp confidence giving way to something quieter, measured. Focused. "This isn't a scouting party," he said.

Gantar inclined his head. "No, it's not," he confirmed. Rain slid from the branches now, steady and cold.

Eldrin exhaled once. "Then we move."

He met Gantar's eyes. The sage studied the treeline for a heartbeat longer than comfort allowed.

"Yes," he said. "Before it's too late."

The forest seemed to lean inward. Somewhere nearby, something breathed, slow, patient, certain. They were being followed. And the storm moved with them.

Whatever hunted them had time. And it intended to use it.

The rain pleased them. It softened the ground, blurred the edges of sound, and swallowed scent. The forest accepted it as camouflage, and the dark elves moved as if they had been born from its roots. They did not hurry or speak.

From a rise overlooking the low trail, Vaelrys, their commander, watched the waystation lights fade behind the trees. Not close enough to be seen. But close enough to feel the pull of what waited there.

Drovane had chosen Vaelrys carefully. She followed orders precisely and thought three moves ahead of the enemy.

The elf with the fire was in the lead. Below her, shapes shifted, scouts repositioning without signal, blades wrapped in dark cloth, bows strung and ready, but never drawn too soon. A net, not a charge.

A young captain stepped to her side, careful not to rise above the rain.

"They've left the road."

Vaelrys nodded once. "As expected."

"They're moving fast."

"Because they know," Vaelrys said. "Not who hunts them. Only that something does."

Vaelrys lowered her hand. Not a signal to advance, only to adjust.

The scouts nearest the trail melted backward into the trees, trading positions with others already moving to flank. No one crossed open ground. Or rushed the distance. The forest itself became their map, every dip and root memorized long before the hunt began.

"They're listening," the young captain murmured. "The one in the middle, he keeps glancing back."

"Good," Vaelrys said. "Fear sharpens patterns."

She watched the riders thread through the undergrowth, careful, but not desperate. They had skill. Discipline. Enough to be dangerous, if this were a fair encounter. It would not be.

"They are headed right where we want them," she continued. Her gaze flicked toward the darker slope ahead, where the land dipped and the trees grew close and old. "The forest tightens there."

The captain nodded. "Do we move to engage?"

Vaelrys's expression did not change. "Not yet." She crouched slightly, palm brushing the wet bark beside her. The tree drank the rain greedily, soundless. So would they.

"We let them choose their ground," she said. "Then we decide whether they leave it."

Below them, a branch snapped, too light to be accidental, too controlled to be careless. Vaelrys smiled faintly. They were close now.

And still, the dark elves waited.

Chapter 14

Drakor did not roar. A lesser dragon might have left in fury. Might have burned the forest in spite and pride. Drakor did neither.

He launched into the sky, leaving the Umbrin behind, and climbed higher than the treeline. Higher than the dark elves' schemes. Into the clouds where sound dissolved and sight blurred, where only the old instincts remained. He rolled his shoulders, ignored the ache that followed, then folded his wings and dropped toward the places where the world still remembered fear.

The scream did not belong to an elf. It came from the cliffs beyond the old ravine, where nests clung to stone like scars. Wyverns, smaller than dragons, faster, less patient, lifted their heads as his shadow passed over them. They knew him. Not as master, but as commander.

He landed hard among the rocks and let his presence unfurl. The air thickened as wings rustled. Yellow eyes blinked open in the dark. Hundreds.

Wyverns did not roar in greeting. They circled and watched. Necks craned, barbed tails flicking against stone as leathery wings folded and unfolded in restless cycles. Scarred hides bore the marks of old battles, burns that had never healed properly, talons broken and reset crooked. Creatures shaped by hunger. And the memory of command.

Drakor lifted his head slowly, letting them see the ruin of him, the torn wing, the darkened scars, the fire that still smoldered behind his eyes. "I do not come to rule you," he said.

A ripple passed through the flock. Low chuffs. The rustle of wings.

"I come to give you prey."

The air shifted, not toward submission, but attention. Heads tilted. Wings stilled. One wyvern stepped forward, larger than the rest, its throat sac scarred and stiff with old burns. Drakor met its gaze.

"The skies are changing," he continued. "Marks have awakened. Songs are being sung again." His lips curled faintly. "And soon, dragons will rise who believe the world belongs to them."

A hiss slithered through the ravine.

"They will need to be reminded," Drakor said softly, "that fear still flies." He spread his wings just enough. Not to threaten. To promise what would follow.

"Fly," he said, voice low and grinding. "Hunt. Scatter what hides."

The wyverns answered. They launched into the rain in ragged waves, shrieking as they climbed, fanning out across the forest's edge toward the waystation.

Drakor watched them rise, satisfaction curling tight and sharp in his chest. Let the elves play at patience, he thought. Let them tighten their nets and whisper their plans.

He would turn the forest into a blade.

The second call went deeper. Into soil long accustomed to blood. Into shadows that did not belong to the night.

Drakor banked south, toward the blackened hollows where the nemods still gathered, fewer now, but no less lethal. They would answer his summons. They followed destruction, craved elven flesh, and lived for death.

Movement stirred below.

He landed hard enough to fracture stone and dug his claws into the earth, letting the scent of old magic bleed into the rain. The sound echoed like bone dragged across bone. Shapes peeled free of the hollows, coalescing into forms only barely bound to flesh. Blades grew where hands should be. Eyes opened where there had been none before.

At their center stood Varagos, the nemod commander, his head tilted as if listening to something beneath the world, something older than Drakor's voice and less inclined to obey it. For a heartbeat too long, he did not move.

Drakor's wings tightened as he growled, "The marked ones scatter and hide. They are divided. We strike now."

A low sound rippled through the gathered nemods, not quite a challenge, not quite assent. Hunger, tempered by something unfamiliar.

Drakor stepped closer, fire bleeding from the scars along his throat. "You hesitate," he said softly. The air around him warped with heat. Rain hissed to steam where it touched his scales.

Varagos's head inclined a fraction. Not assent. Calculation.

Drakor's rage surged as a roar split the hollow, shattering rock and scattering the smaller forms. Flame erupted in a violent arc, carving a warning into the stone at Varagos's feet. "You do not question," Drakor snarled. "You do not wait. You ride. Toward the waystation."

Silence slammed back into place.

"Now!" roared Drakor, his tail slamming the ground, sending loose rocks and debris flying.

Varagos turned at last, a single sharp gesture sending the order rippling outward. The nemods mounted their dark nightmares, creatures bred for terror and speed, and melted into the trees like a spreading stain.

Drakor watched them go, fury simmering beneath his scales. “Ride,” he murmured, voice edged with promise and threat alike. “Ride and flush them toward fate.”

The forest swallowed them whole. And somewhere far ahead, the marked ones kept running, unaware that the darkness behind them had just been taught how to obey again.

Drakor rose once more, wings beating hard against the storm. Far below, the forest shifted. Not with panic. With inevitability.

Birds scattered. Small beasts fled downslope. The world began to fray, not broken yet, but bent. The darkness moved, swift now. Purposeful.

Nemods slipped through the trees, the forest yielding to their passage as though it remembered them. Wyverns gathered in the storm clouds, shapes multiplying as the sky darkened. Soon they would swarm whatever stood in their way, dark or not.

Drakor watched, satisfaction coiling tight in his chest. Let the dark elves play their clever games. Let them weave their nets. He would drown the board in blood.

But beneath the hunger and the rage, something else lingered. A pressure, vast and old, pressing upward through stone and root and buried fire.

His breath caught for half a heartbeat. He licked the wind, tasting the air. Something stirred beneath the world... and he would have to find it.

Before it found him.

The edges of his maw curved upward as he banked sharply, not toward the forest, not toward the hunt, but toward what was rising to meet him.

Chapter 15

The council chamber had never felt so hollow. Polished and bare, the long table stretched beneath guttering torches along the walls, their flames bending whenever the wind pressed against the high windows. Banners hung motionless, too motionless, bearing the sigils of ancient houses that had once spoken with a single voice. Now, they waited.

King Eldermyst stood at the head of the table, hands braced against the carved oak, his reflection fractured across the polished surface. Dawn filtered weakly through the upper windows, catching the silver threads in his hair and the deep lines carved by sleepless nights.

Gantar's seat was empty. So was Thalendir's. That absence weighed more heavily than any accusation ever had.

Lady Alariel broke the silence first, as she always did. "We cannot delay this council any longer," she said, fingers folded neatly atop her notes. "The disturbances along our borders grow more frequent. Storms. Unnatural movements. Whispers from the outer woods."

Elder Faelorn inclined his head. "The forest confirms it. Roots recoil. Birds abandon their nests. The land itself senses imbalance."

"And yet," Lord Thalion said, arms crossed over his armor, voice hard, "we still lack proof of intent. Or enemy."

Eldermyst did not look at him. Proof, he thought bitterly, had never stopped fear from spreading.

Lady Seraphina shifted in her chair. "Our kingdom grows uneasy," she said carefully. "Silence breeds suspicion. They ask why Gantar has not spoken. Why the king's sons are no longer seen."

Lord Thalion's gaze hardened. "Unease does not rise without cause. Our borders do not stir on their own." His eyes flicked, briefly, deliberately, to the empty seat where Gantar and Thalendir should have been. "Nor do our princes vanish without influence."

Eldermyst straightened slowly, the movement controlled, but only just. "My sons," he said, voice low, "are not council property."

A ripple moved through the chamber. Not dissent, uncertainty.

Elder Sylthir leaned forward, eyes sharp beneath the shadow of his hood. "No," he agreed softly. "But absence invites... contingency."

His fingers steepled. "We have seen this pattern before," he said quietly. "A voice that does not sound like an enemy. A cause that cloaks itself in need." His gaze slid toward the window, toward the mountains beyond. "It did not end well for us," he continued, "when one of our own mistook the enemy for something worthy of love... and paid the price alone."

The king's hands tightened on the table. Oak creaked. "No," Eldermyst said, too fast this time, the word cutting sharper than intended. He straightened fully now, no longer bracing himself. "Do not dare," he said, voice rising for the first time, "to cloak your fear in memory you do not carry."

The torches guttered as his power flared, subtle, restrained, but undeniable. "That wound did not belong to this council," he went on. "It belonged to my family." Eldermyst finally turned, his gaze finding Sylthir's without flinching. "Say what you mean."

Sylthir did not smile. "The realm watches you, my king. And wonders whether loyalty still outweighs prophecy."

Silence followed. Not the charged fury of the last council Gantar had faced, but something colder. Calculation.

Lady Alariel cleared her throat. "The matter before us," she said, "is not blame. It is governance. Gantar has vanished. Eldrin defied tradition. Thalendir followed, or disappeared attempting to prevent it."

"Whatever guides them," Lady Alariel continued carefully, "did not arise from within our halls."

The words were measured. And unmistakable.

Elder Faelorn shifted. "Be wary of old conclusions," he warned. "The land recoils from division as sharply as it does from shadow." His voice dropped. "And the storms answer no law we recognize."

"The land does not sit this council," Thalion replied. "We do."

Eldermyst felt the fracture then, not as a sudden break, but as a slow, spreading fault beneath stone. He knew Gantar had to move unseen. He felt Eldrin's need to follow the prophecy. To honor his mother's memory. And he respected Thalendir's choice to accompany his brother.

He told himself he could hold the council together. Despite circumstances. He had been wrong.

"Enough!" he said. The chamber stilled, not because of authority alone, but because of the weight behind the word. "I will not condemn my sons in absentia," Eldermyst continued. "Nor will I pretend ignorance of forces older than this council's memory."

Sylthir watched him closely. "Then you admit the prophecy guides them."

"I admit," the king said evenly, "that the prophecy has always guided us. Whether we wished it or not."

"And it has led us astray before," Sylthir said softly.

Eldermyst's jaw tightened. He did not deny it. "Yes," Eldermyst said, eyes blazing now, "the prophecy has led us astray."

He took a breath, slow, deliberate. "And it has saved us. Repeatedly. Quietly. At cost." His gaze swept the table. "You speak of deception as though it were a single sin. I tell you, this realm survives because some dared to believe when certainty failed."

Lord Thalion's jaw tightened. "My king, I fear we stand at the edge of war. Uncertain of our true enemy."

Eldermyst met his gaze. "Then we prepare our borders quietly," he said. "And we seek allies. If this is war, all realms stand to lose, and the prophecy may be the only path left to us." His eyes moved around the table, measured and unyielding. One by one, the councilors broke his gaze.

Not in defiance. In unease.

Lady Seraphina nodded at once. "Discretion preserves alliances," she said. "If aid must be accepted beyond our borders, it is best done without spectacle."

The word *aid* landed harder than steel.

Lady Alariel's fingers stilled above her notes. "And if that aid comes from those we once cast out?" she asked carefully. "Will the realm understand such silence, or mistake it for weakness?"

Lord Thalion's voice hardened. "Our borders exist for a reason."

Elder Faelorn bowed his head. "So do wounds," he murmured. "And some never healed cleanly."

No one answered him.

Elder Sylthir smiled, just faintly. "Then we agree on one thing," he breathed. "This is no longer a question of defense." His gaze swept the table. "But whether we bind ourselves to those the prophecy has already touched."

Lady Alariel's voice was calm. "There are alliances this realm cannot survive."

A murmur moved across the table. Heads inclined. Fingers tightened against wood.

Lord Thalion nodded once. "I will not bind elven steel to drelf blood."

The words settled heavily in the chamber.

Eldermyst felt it then. Eyes that would not meet his. Chairs shifting. Throats clearing.

Some waited. Some recoiled. And some had already closed the door.

The council was no longer deciding how to prepare. They were deciding who would never be trusted. Some feared invasion. Others feared truth. And some feared neither, only the cost of admitting they had been wrong.

Beyond the windows, the wind rose, not in answer, but in warning. Far from banners and law, forces were already moving. For the first time since ascending the throne, King Eldermyst understood the truth Gantar had never spoken aloud:

The realm did not fear darkness. It feared being wrong again, about what it did not understand, what it had chosen to believe, and the ones it had blamed.

Chapter 16

The chamber emptied slowly. Not in argument. Not in protest. Just in careful steps and lowered voices, as though sound itself might carry consequence.

King Eldermyst remained. When the doors finally closed, the echo lingered longer than it should have. He stood where he had stood through the council's fracture, hands resting on the table's edge, the carved oak still bearing the faint impressions of his grip.

The banners stirred as the wind slipped through the upper windows, restless, insistent. Gantar would have waited. Not out of fear. Out of patience.

Eldermyst closed his eyes. *And patience,* he thought, *is no longer enough.*

He crossed the chamber and moved through a narrow side passage known only to a few, a relic of older kings and quieter wars. It opened onto a balcony overlooking the eastern forests, where dawn had thinned the night.

The land looked unchanged. That was the lie of it. Storms brewed beyond the horizon. He felt it in the air, in the way the wind tugged at his cloak as though urging him forward. Somewhere beyond the trees, his sons walked paths he could not follow. Somewhere farther still, a kingdom his realm had named enemy carried a truth the realm would soon need, whether it dared to face it or not.

The council would debate. They would stall. They would demand proof. They would cloak fear in caution and call it wisdom while the realms burned.

Eldermyst's hand drifted to the ring on his finger, Thariel's, worn thin with age and memory. She had believed in quiet courage. Not the kind that announced itself. The kind that acted when others hesitated.

His thoughts shifted to another presence entirely. Not as the council remembered her, but as she had been before the exile. Before the lie. Before the realm had chosen certainty over truth and paid for it in blood and centuries of denial.

We failed you, he thought. His head lowered, his throat tightening. *I failed... both of you.*

And now, if he waited for permission to do what must be done, he would fail again. There would be nothing left to save. Nothing left to remember. The prophecy did not demand obedience. It demanded choice.

Eldermyst straightened. When he turned from the balcony, his decision was already made.

Master Trainer Aldareth did not ask why. That was why Eldermyst trusted him. The older elf stood at the training hall's shadowed edge, arms folded, eyes sharp despite the early hour. The sounds of steel rang faintly from the lower yards, routine drills unchanged by councils or prophecy.

Aldareth inclined his head. "You'll have resistance."

"I know."

"And consequence."

"Yes. And by the time the council realizes what I have done, they will already be there."

Aldareth reached into his cloak and produced a folded parchment. Not sealed. Not ceremonial. Names. No ranks. No titles.

Some Eldermyst expected. Others surprised him.

"Loyalists," Aldareth said quietly. "Scouts. Wardens from the outer woods. And elves who will fight to keep their families safe."

Eldermyst nodded. "Enough?"

"For what you intend?" Aldareth met his gaze. "Yes."

Eldermyst allowed himself a single, grim breath. "Very well."

Aldareth's mouth curved, not quite a smile. "Then we move quietly."

Borders would be reinforced. Patrols doubled without banners raised. Messengers sent north, not as heralds, but as envoys.

Not an army. A gesture. A risk.

Eldermyst folded the list and slipped it into his sleeve. "Prepare them," he said. "And Aldareth..."

"Yes, my king."

"If this fails," Eldermyst said, voice steady, "history will not be kind."

Aldareth's answer was immediate. "History never is."

The king watched him go. Beyond stone walls and ancient law, the wind rose again, carrying with it the echo of wings not yet seen. And far from councils and crowns, the prophecy continued to move. Not because it was commanded. But because someone had finally chosen to listen.

Chapter 17

The rain came down harder now, drops pooling along the trail, turning earth to slick mud beneath the horses' hooves. Their tracks would show, clearer with every step, the outlines of hooves drawing a map no one in this forest would mistake.

Branches tore at cloaks and packs as Eldrin drove them downslope through the trees, horses skidding on wet stone, breath held tight against the cold. The forest no longer whispered. It rushed past in broken gasps, leaves bending, undergrowth parting too cleanly behind them. Eldrin did not recognize the land or the trail beneath it. But whatever followed moved as if it had walked it before.

At his back, silver light bled through the rain as the marks at Finnian's temples flared again, uneven, casting an eerie shimmer that pulsed once, then steadied.

Eldrin glanced back. "Finn, do you recognize this trail?"

Finnian opened his mouth, then stopped. His brow furrowed, breath hitching as the silver light at his temples flickered again, dim this time. Uncertain. "I..." He swallowed. "I should. It feels... familiar. But it's not lining up."

The delay was enough. A sound shifted somewhere downslope, not close, but closer than it had been. Thalendir reined in beside Eldrin. "We should cut east," he said. "Higher ground. We can force them to spread."

Eldrin looked where Thalendir indicated. The Aetherstone lay still at his side. He shook his head. "No. They'll expect that."

Thalendir frowned. "You're guessing."

Eldrin tightened his grip on the reins. "So are they." He turned. "Gantar?"

The sage did not look back. "We keep moving."

They pressed on.

At first, nothing seemed wrong. The ground sloped steadily downward, roots slick with rain, stones half-buried beneath leaf rot. Eldrin leaned into the rhythm of the rain, trusting muscle memory where thought would slow him. Then the forest changed. Not abruptly. Not enough to name. Sound dulled first, the thunder of hooves flattening into something muted, swallowed.

Finnian frowned, fingers flexing against the reins as if testing the air itself. "Hold..." he began.

Too late.

The ground ahead dipped sharply, then gave, not collapsing, but yielding in a way soil should not. Silverwind skidded, hooves scrabbling for purchase before Eldrin hauled her sideways, barely keeping them upright. Behind him, Embermane stumbled hard, Finnian swearing as he fought for balance.

Thalendir spun in his saddle. "That wasn't there."

"It was," Aelar said, breath tight. "Just... not like that."

Rain slid off the leaves in thin, whispering sheets. The trees leaned closer together here, trunks bent at unfamiliar angles, branches crossing overhead like ribs.

Finnian pressed a hand to his temples, face pale. The marks glimmered faintly, uneven, unstable. "I can't..." He shook his head. "It's not lining up anymore. Every direction feels... crowded."

Another sound carried through the trees. Closer now. Eldrin could feel the failure of the path itself. Whatever hunted them was no longer following the ground. It was following intent.

"Gantar," Eldrin said, quieter now. "This isn't working."

The sage slowed. He reined in slightly, his mount restless beneath him. He did not look back down the trail. Instead, his gaze lifted, scanning the warped angles of the forest ahead, not searching, not listening, but remembering.

"Yes," he said. "They've learned how we choose."

Thalendir leaned closer in the saddle, voice tight. "Then tell us which way to go."

Gantar hesitated. Just long enough to make Eldrin's chest tighten. "There are places," the sage said at last, voice low, "where pursuit falters."

The forest answered his words. Not with sound, but with presence.

Eldrin caught the first glimpse between the trees: a shape where no shape should have been. A figure half-veiled in bark-shadow, then gone. Watching.

Another appeared farther upslope. Then another.

Dark elves moved through the forest like thought itself, silent, spaced, never close enough to challenge, never far enough to lose. They did not rush, or signal. They closed.

Finnian sucked in a breath. "That's why," he said hoarsely. "That's why it feels wrong. They're not behind us. They're all around us."

As if in answer, something snorted low and wet from the brush below. Silverwind shied, ears flattening. Embermane stamped, nostrils flaring as a stench cut through the rain, something feral beneath it.

Nemods. Their Shadowmanes slunk through the undergrowth, barely visible except where rain beaded along slick, unnatural hides. They did not bark or howl. They scented.

Aelar's blade slid free with a whisper. "They've got ground and shadow."

"And sky," Thalendir said.

Eldrin followed his gaze.

The rain thinned overhead, just enough to see the shapes circling above the canopy, wide-winged silhouettes drifting against the bruised sky. Wyverns. Not diving. Not calling. Waiting.

The pressure slammed into Finnian all at once. He gasped, clutching his temples as silver light flared, spilling across the rain like shattered moonlight. "There's no space," he choked. "They've filled it. Every direction, it's all occupied."

Gantar's jaw tightened. "A complete net."

The dark elves shifted again, closer now. Nemods crept forward, claws sinking soundlessly into mud. Above them, the wyverns dipped, tightening their circles.

Eldrin felt the weight of it then, not fear, but choice collapsing. Behind them, pursuit. Around them, containment. Above them, patience.

He looked ahead, toward the warped treeline, where the forest bent inward, where sound already behaved wrong and the air felt thick with unspoken memory.

Gantar's voice cut through the rain, sharp with urgency as he pointed ahead. "There, Eldrin. Now."

Eldrin did not question it. They spurred forward as one, breaking toward the only ground that had not yet yielded to prediction. The earth vanished.

Silverwind screamed as the forest floor gave way beneath her hooves, stone and root peeling back to reveal open sky below. The world tipped, gravity tearing free as they plunged through mist and echo.

Wind roared upward, warm, ancient, carrying the scent of stone and wing. Then light rose to meet them. Not from above, from below. The forest remembered, and the Well of Wings opened.

They did not land. They were caught. The fall slowed without warning, speed bleeding away as if the air itself had thickened, mist curling around them like unseen hands. Wind softened. Gravity loosened its grip. What should have been impact became suspension. Hooves touched stone. Not hard, or soft. Simply there.

Silverwind stumbled once, then steadied, snorting sharply as steam rose from her flanks, her hide quivering beneath the saddle. The echo of her landing stretched too long, then thinned into nothing at all. They had entered the Well as sound unraveled around them.

Above, the rain faded, not stopping, but losing relevance, as though it belonged to a world no longer present. Hoofbeats echoed once, twice, then refused to carry. Even breath felt reluctant to travel far.

Eldrin slowed, lifting a hand. This place was not a refuge. It was a question.

Finnian swayed in his saddle, one hand rising instinctively to his temples, breath shallow. Beneath him, Embermane stilled. The buckskin lowered his head, nostrils flaring as he sniffed the stone beneath his hooves. His ears flicked forward, then back, muscles bunching tight beneath his hide, as if weighing whether to advance or bolt.

The Well opened around them in slow degrees, as though it had no interest in being seen all at once. Stone curved where it should have fallen away, walls arching high and wide, etched with veins that caught no light yet seemed to remember it. The floor beneath them was smooth and ancient.

Far above, or perhaps far below, the space widened into shadow, depth impossible to measure. Sound did not echo so much as sink, swallowed the moment it was made.

Gantar did not look around at all. His eyes were closed. "We are inside it now," the sage said quietly.

"Inside what?" Eldrin asked.

Gantar nodded, but did not open his eyes.

"Where are we, Gantar?" Finnian asked.

Gantar exhaled slowly. "That depends," he said.

"On what?" Eldrin asked.

"On whether you mean where your feet stand," Gantar replied, "or where your memories do."

Somewhere beneath their feet, deep enough that stone forgot its own name, something shifted.

And the dagger at Eldrin's side glowed blue.

Chapter 18

Nyxari was already in the room.

Fizzlewing froze mid-hover, glow flaring bright gold in alarm. “I told you she invited me,” he said faintly.

Lyria had not moved. She sat upright on the bed, hand pressed flat against her chest where the ache had settled deeper than breath.

Nyxari stood at the foot of the bed, bone-and-crystal charms drifting around her, their threads overlapping where they should not. They trembled. The Seer’s gaze never left Lyria. “You feel it,” she said quietly.

Lyria swallowed. “I don’t know what it is.”

“It is many things,” Nyxari said.

Kaelis stepped closer, placing herself in front of Lyria. “What’s happening?”

Nyxari’s eyes flicked to her, measuring, respectful. “A dragon stirs,” she said. “And your friends are headed toward danger.”

Lyria's breath caught. The ache in her chest sharpened. And for a heartbeat, it felt almost familiar.

Nyxari lowered her hand, and the charms stilled. "They have entered the place that remembers," she said and turned toward the narrow window where the mountains cut dark shapes against the thinning night. "It is time, Lyria," Nyxari said. "For you to answer the mark."

Lyria rose to her feet. "What about the council?" she asked.

Nyxari did not hesitate. "I will handle them."

Lyria tilted her head, studying the Seer's face. "They won't like being left in the dark."

"They rarely do," Nyxari replied calmly. "But they hear what they are ready to hear. No more. No less."

The two drelves regarded one another in silence. Years of shared history passed between them, debate, defiance, trust earned the hard way. At last, Nyxari stepped forward and placed a steady hand on Lyria's shoulder.

Lyria exhaled slowly and nodded.

Kaelis did not move. "Wait," she said. "You want her to do what?" Her voice was steady, but there was iron beneath it now.

Nyxari turned back from the window. "I am not asking," she said. "I am witnessing."

"That's not the same thing," Kaelis shot back. "You see threads. You feel echoes. But she bleeds." Kaelis's hand came to rest lightly at Lyria's back, a familiar anchor. "She has already paid for things she never chose."

The charms stirred again, softly this time. Nyxari regarded Kaelis for a long moment. Not with impatience. With something closer to sorrow. "You think I do not know that?" she asked. "You think I have not watched this realm ask the innocent to carry what the guilty buried?"

"Then stop it," Kaelis said. "For once. Stop letting the world take from her."

Silence settled between them.

Nyxari inclined her head, just slightly. "If I could, I would."

Kaelis's jaw tightened. "That's not an answer."

"It is the only honest one."

Lyria felt the ache pulse again, not sharper, not louder, but deeper. It did not pull her away from Kaelis. It pulled through her.

"She's not choosing this," Kaelis said, more quietly now. "It's choosing her."

Nyxari's gaze softened. "Yes."

Kaelis turned to Lyria then, searching her face, her eyes, her breath, the small, familiar tells she had learned long before wings, before marks, before prophecy. "You don't have to go," she said. "Say the word, and we stay. We hide. We fight our way out if we have to."

Lyria met her gaze. "I know," she said.

Kaelis swallowed hard. "Then why..."

"Because we can't stop what is coming," Lyria said gently. "But maybe we can choose what it becomes."

Kaelis closed her eyes. Just for a heartbeat. When she opened them, something had shifted, not acceptance, but resolve. "Then I'm going with you," she said flatly.

Nyxari did not object. She only watched.

Fizzlewing cleared his throat loudly. "Just for the record," he said, puffing himself up, "I'm coming too."

Kaelis huffed a breath that might have been a laugh. Lyria reached for Kaelis's hand, and her friend laced their fingers together without hesitation.

Nyxari's mouth curved, not quite a smile. She stepped back, already turning toward the door. "Gather what you need," she said. "We move now." She paused only long enough to add, "Zeynar will follow."

The charms stilled.

Lyria did not know where she was going. Only that she had to go.

Chapter 19

The air changed before Lyria saw it. Her wings slowed as the mountains opened beneath her, jagged silhouettes cutting into the dawn. The wind no longer pushed, it guided, curling around her as if testing her intent.

Kaelis flew close at her side, silent now, her usual sharpness subdued by the way the air pressed in on them. Zeynar followed just behind, his wings beating slow and measured, eyes scanning the stone and sky with equal caution. Even Fizzlewing had stopped chattering, his glow dimmed to a soft, wary gold as he hovered near Lyria's shoulder.

Ahead, the mountains folded inward. Stone rose in overlapping arcs, ancient and worn, forming an arch where wind and sound bent strangely, refusing to carry the way they should. The Well of Wings.

Lyria did not know how she knew the name. Only that it settled into her bones as if it had always been there. She angled downward, wings catching the air with careful precision as she descended toward the place where stone and ground met. The closer she came, the stronger the pull became, not dragging her forward, but inviting.

Below them, the Well waited.

And as Lyria passed over the opening, something deep within the mountains shifted. Stone rose on either side of them, not sheer, not smooth, layered, as though the mountain had folded in on itself and never fully unfolded again.

Wind slid through the Well in uneven currents, tugging at wings as they landed. "I've been here before," Lyria breathed. "A long time ago."

Kaelis nodded. "It's where Nyxari found us."

Lyria's chest tightened. She turned toward Kaelis, measuring, searching, but Kaelis had already stepped ahead. The air changed again. Heavier this time, like a breath the world had been holding.

Lyria's feet moved closer to the Well, heart pounding. She did not know what drew her to the stone wall, only that her hand lifted before thought caught up. Her fingers brushed over carved letters half-worn by time. The word pulsed faintly beneath her touch. Kaelis reached out. Their hands met, tracing the letters together.

Ironwing.

Fizzlewing inhaled sharply. "Oh," he whispered.

They all turned toward him.

"That name," he said, glow brightening despite himself, "is... older than drelves. Older than elves." He drifted closer to the stone, careful not to touch it. "It's in the songs. The ancient ones, that no one wants to remember."

Zeynar's gaze sharpened. "Go on..."

Fizzlewing swallowed. "Ironwing comes from the original song. A verse, wings of iron, foretelling the marked one who would come bearing power. Not born of one realm. Not claimed by one voice." He glanced at Lyria. "Someone the mountain itself would recognize."

Silence pressed in.

Lyria's pulse thundered in her ears. "It's just my name," she said, quietly, uncertain.

Fizzlewing shook his head. "No. It's the name the Well remembers."

The stone beneath Lyria's palm warmed, just slightly.

Zeynar bowed his head, not deeply, not ceremonially. Just enough. "The mountain does not carve lightly," he said.

"He's right," said the sprite. "That is a name that echoed down the Well, into the realms, until drelves learned to speak it again."

Lyria drew a steady breath. She understood now. The Well had spoken her name first. And it had been waiting for her to answer. She knew now why the giants had heard her name. Why the elves had feared it. And why the dragons had tried to silence it.

Ironwing was never meant to belong to the past. It was meant to endure, and bring forth what came next. Somewhere deep beneath the Well, something ancient shifted, listening. Waiting. For the one who bore the name to choose what it would become.

Eldrin felt it before he saw her. Not a presence, but a weight settling into its balance. The Aetherstone at his side warmed, not with warning, not with urgency, but with recognition. As though something long misaligned had finally found its axis.

He turned to look upward. The Well lay open beneath the sky, its vast stone ring holding silence like a vow. The wind moved differently there, circling, listening, unwilling to rush.

And at its edge, a drelf stood. Wings half-furled. Spine straight. Feet planted as though the ground itself had claimed her.

Lyria.

Eldrin did not move. Because something in her had changed. Not her stance. Not her strength. Her gravity.

Lyria gazed, not at him, not at anyone, but at the rock, at the carved wall curving along the Well's inner rim. Her hand rose slowly as she touched the stone. "Ironwing," she said. Not questioning its significance this time, but accepting it.

The word settled into the air, not loudly, not dramatically, but with the quiet finality of truth reclaimed. Kaelis sucked in a sharp breath behind her.

Finnian's mark stirred, not burning this time, but listening, as though a voice had recognized its own heart.

Gantar bowed his head. So, this was it. Not the end, but the beginning that was foretold.

Lyria turned then, just enough for Eldrin to see her profile, the strength in her jaw, the steadiness in her eyes. She did not look at him or see him. But she no longer felt lost, or cursed.

And Eldrin understood with a clarity that hurt.

She had found the place where she left herself.

Chapter 20

He tasted it first on his tongue. The shift in the air. Bitter. Metallic. Not smoke, not magic, memory. It clung to the back of his throat, thin as ash, and Drakor knew at once what it was not. It was not the Abyss. Not Vartharax.

He lifted his head slowly, scarred neck plates grinding as the wind slid across his fangs. This was older than fear. Quieter than rage. And it was waking.

Drakor's mouth curved into a thin, uneasy smile. "So," he breathed. "It's you..."

He banked sharply, not toward the forest, not toward the hunt, but toward what was rising to meet him. The storm thinned as he climbed, clouds tearing apart beneath the force of his wings.

Below him, the land grew barren, color draining from soil and stone alike. Forests gave way to exposed rock, where life pulled back. The wind changed. It carried bone, ash, and the echo of wings that would never rise again.

The Dragon Graveyard.

Drakor did not slow. The place loomed ahead, vast and sunken, a wound in the world where the mountains themselves had collapsed inward. Spines of stone jutted from the earth like ribs. Half-buried skeletons sprawled across the basin, their scale plates dulled to chalk and rust, wings shattered where they had fallen. Dragons who had battled, and lost.

Drakor descended through the thinning mist, landing hard among the remains. The ground trembled beneath his weight, loose fragments of bone skittering across the stone. The presence was stronger here. He could feel it beneath the earth.

Drakor inhaled slowly, fire stirring behind his ribs. His gaze swept the graveyard, narrowing. "Show yourself," he growled, not as an order, but as a challenge.

The wind moved through the bones, over stone and ash. But nothing answered.

"I know you're here," he said, and the graveyard did not disagree.

His claws curled as the stone beneath his feet warmed. Not with fire. With recognition.

Drakor stilled. This place was dead. It remembered only endings. Victory had never belonged here. And yet, beneath the ash and splintered bone, the ground answered him not with fear, but with awareness.

A low vibration threaded through the basin. Too slow to be sound. Too deep to be felt through flesh alone. Drakor's wings twitched, half-spreading before he forced them still.

The wind shifted again, circling, not around him, but around a point deeper in the graveyard. Somewhere beneath collapsed stone and layers of dragons who would never rise again. There. Faint. Weak. But there.

Drakor exhaled through his teeth. His gaze sharpened, tracking the pull beneath the earth, the subtle tilt in the air, the way ash lifted and settled as though breathing.

She had not returned yet. But she was remembering how. And that meant time was shorter than he'd planned.

Something deep beneath the stone shifted again. And for the first time in a very long while, Drakor felt it, the prickle of a future he did not control.

Chapter 21

The council chamber was already full when King Eldermyst entered. Too full. Not with voices, but with expectation. The kind that pressed down on the shoulders and made even seasoned lords measure their breath. News had traveled ahead of him. It always did.

He did not take the high seat at once. That alone unsettled them.

"I have acted," Eldermyst said, before any formal greeting could be spoken.

A ripple moved through the chamber.

"I have sent envoys beyond our borders," he continued. "To the mountains."

Silence hardened. Lady Alariel's fingers tightened on the edge of the table. Lord Thalion's jaw set.

"You did so without council sanction," one voice said.

"Yes," Eldermyst replied evenly. "Because sanction would have come too late."

Elder Sylthir leaned forward, eyes sharp. "Then say it plainly, my king."

Eldermyst met his gaze. "I have sought alliance with the drelves."

The chamber fractured. Not into shouting, but into lines.

"You would bind elven fate to exile?" Thalion demanded.

Eldermyst did not flinch. "No," he said. "I would bind it to truth."

The council chamber did not erupt. That was what troubled Eldermyst most. No shouts. No outrage. Only the slow, collective stilling of bodies that recognized a line had been crossed and could not yet decide whether to step back from it.

"You have acted without leave," Lord Thalion said at last.

"Yes," Eldermyst replied. "I have."

Lady Alariel's fingers folded together. "Then we must ask why."

Eldermyst moved forward at last, resting his hands on the table, not in supplication, but in ownership. "Because waiting has become a choice," he said. "And every choice we have made so far has led us here."

Elder Sylthir's eyes narrowed. "You speak as though the council bears blame."

"I speak as though the realm does," Eldermyst answered calmly. "Myself included."

That unsettled them more than anger would have.

"The drelves are not allies," Thalion said. "They are descendants of exile."

"Yes," Eldermyst agreed. "And we are descendants of the decision that made them so."

A murmur stirred, uneasy, restrained. Lady Seraphina leaned forward. "You would reopen wounds we sealed generations ago."

"No," Eldermyst said. "We only pretended they healed."

Silence fell harder this time.

"The prophecy stirs," he continued. "Not as weapon. Not as threat. But as reckoning. And my sons, both of them, stand within its turning."

A sharp inhale. A chair scraped faintly against stone.

"You risk the heirs," someone said.

"I risk the realm," Eldermyst corrected. "Because the prophecy does not spare us for refusing to see it."

Elder Faelorn spoke quietly. "You believe the marks cannot stand alone."

"I know they cannot," Eldermyst said. "Not divided. Not mistrusted. Not built on the same lie that broke the Covenant the first time."

Sylthir's gaze sharpened. "Then tell us, my king, what lie is that?"

Eldermyst met his eyes. "We sent her away because we were afraid."

The chamber stilled. Not even breath moved.

"We feared what love might cost us," Eldermyst continued. "What unity might demand. And so, we chose certainty over truth and taught our children to call that wisdom."

He let the silence stretch. "That choice," he said quietly, "took my wife from me."

A stir moved through the chamber. Eldermyst did not raise his voice. "Thariel believed in the Covenant," he continued. "Not as doctrine. As responsibility. She believed that what was broken could still be mended, if someone was willing to pay the cost."

Lord Thalion shifted. "No one denies your loss, my king..."

"I am not asking it to be denied," Eldermyst said. "I am stating it." His gaze swept the table. "The exile did not only birth another realm. It hollowed this one. It taught us to fear connection and then punished those who refused to obey that fear."

He did not say Thariel's name again. He did not need to.

Lady Alariel's voice was very soft. "You speak of ancient matters."

"I speak of a choice that still governs us," Eldermyst replied. "A lie that hardened into law."

Thalion's hand clenched on the table. "You would condemn our ancestors."

"No," Eldermyst said. "I would stop hiding behind them."

The words rang, not loud, but absolute.

"The prophecy does not ask us to rule," he continued. "It asks us to remember. To unite what fear divided. And whether we approve or not, the drelves are already part of that convergence."

Elder Faelorn bowed his head. "The land has been telling us this for years."

Sylthir watched Eldermyst carefully. "Then this meeting is not to ask permission."

Eldermyst did not hesitate. "No. It is merely to inform you," he said. "I have already acted. As king. As father. As one who remembers what the Covenant was."

That fractured the room at last. Not into chaos, but into truth. Some stood, others remained seated or looked away, not in defiance, but in recognition of what they could not yet accept.

Eldermyst straightened. "I have offered alliance," he said. The king looked around the chamber, his gaze settling on each council member in turn. "The drelves are already moving, and if they accept it, we will move with them."

No one spoke.

"Those who will stand with me," Eldermyst said, voice steady, "stand now. Those who will not, do not mistake hesitation for wisdom."

Outside, the wind rose, not violently, but with purpose. The council had not unified. But the realm had moved. And far beyond stone walls and ancient law, forces were already turning toward the Well.

They did not cross a border marked by stone or banner. The land simply changed as the air thinned, trees grew sparse, and the mountains rose, not as shelter, but as judgment. The elven envoys reined in as one, their horses uneasy beneath them, ears flicking at sounds that did not behave like echoes.

A figure detached from the stone ahead. Winged, with padded feet and armored skin. Steel whispered free of its sheath. The blade did not tremble. Behind him, the forest shifted, not with movement, but presence. Bowstrings drew back without sound. Shadows resolved into shapes: wings folded tight, talons braced against stone and bark. Drelves emerged from places the eye refused to remember as empty.

"You are far from home," the drelf said. The sword remained leveled, its edge aimed not at the envoy's heart, but at the space where choice still lived.

"We come at the command of King Eldermyst," the captain said. "Of the Elven Realm."

"State your purpose," the drelf continued. "Quickly."

"We seek audience with those who still remember what the realms once promised each other."

The drelf did not answer at once. His grip shifted, subtle, almost imperceptible, but the blade lowered a fraction, no longer aimed at the envoy's chest. Behind him, wings adjusted. The bowstrings did not slacken, but they did not tighten further either.

The drelf inhaled slowly, tasting the air. "You speak of promises," he said at last. "Elves remember vows only when they are threatened."

The blade dipped another inch. "But you did not come with banners or horns." His gaze flicked briefly, just once, over the elves' small number, their lack of armor, the absence of any war mark.

"You came with words." He turned then, not his back, not fully away, but enough. "Follow," he said.

The surrounding shadows shifted, opening a narrow path between stone and root. Drelves did not vanish. They moved, reforming ahead and behind, enclosing the envoys without touching them.

The drelf glanced back once. "Any blade raised without cause," he said evenly, "will be answered."

Then he stepped forward.

And the mountain closed around them.

Nyxari stilled. The charms at her wrists stirred. Not all at once. First one, then another. Then three more, threads pulling taut in directions that had not aligned in centuries. She exhaled. "So... the king acts at last." Not with force, but with humility.

She felt the choice ripple outward, not loud enough to announce itself, but strong enough to alter what came next. Old resentments flexed. Old wounds tested. The realm did not heal, but it did not refuse.

The stone beneath her feet trembled from something far deeper. Her head lifted. The dragon had stirred again. Not fully risen. But no longer dreaming.

The pulse rolled through the unseen places of the world, through bone and memory, through fire long banked beneath ash. It brushed her senses like a second heartbeat, steady and deliberate.

Her fingers closed around the oldest charm, the one she had never named. "The third remembers," she whispered.

Wind moved across the mountain then, not forward, not back, but sideways. Toward the Well. Toward convergence.

Nyxari turned at last, wings folding close. "The balance tips," she said to the empty air. "And now," she added, voice quiet but unyielding, "the world must answer."

Chapter 22

The first wyvern broke the cloud cover shrieking. Its shadow tore across the stone as it dove, wings snapping the air apart, followed by another, and another, until the sky above the Well was alive with movement.

Nemods poured from the shadowed approaches, their forms half-smoke, half-flesh, blades already drawn. Dark elves followed close behind, feet striking stone in disciplined rhythm, eyes cold and intent.

Lyria felt it immediately, the way space vanished. The slow, deliberate tightening of a noose. Kaelis spun, blades already in her hands. "Sky's gone," she snapped. "And ground's about to be."

A wyvern screamed again, closer this time. Wind slammed down into the basin as it banked, claws raking stone, testing distance. Another circled wide, patient. Waiting for the net to finish closing. Zeynar stepped forward, shield angling instinctively toward the nearest nemods.

Lyria's attention locked, not on the enemies, not on the sky, but on the stone beneath her feet. The Well was no longer still. The air around it thickened, bending strangely, sound dulling at the edges. Ash lifted and settled in slow, spiraling patterns that had nothing to do with the wind. The name carved into the stone pulsed faintly beneath the surface, as if breathing.

Ironwing.

A nemod shrieked as it lunged forward. Kaelis moved without hesitation, blades flashing as she intercepted, steel ringing sharp against corrupted metal. Zeynar advanced in tandem, shield slamming into another creature with bone-jarring force. But there were too many. More poured from the shadows. Wyverns dipped lower, tightening their circles. Dark elves spread wide, bows raised.

Fizzlewing hovered close to Lyria's shoulder, his glow flaring bright and uneven. "This is bad," he said faintly. "This is very, very..."

"Lyria!" a voice shouted from below.

Her gaze followed the sound. Eldrin's.

Kaelis followed her gaze and froze. "No," she said immediately. "We don't know what's down there."

"We know what's up here," Zeynar said grimly, blocking another nemod strike.

A wyvern screamed again, too close. The ground shuddered as one landed hard on the far rim of the basin, talons cracking stone. Its head lowered, eyes burning sulfur-yellow as it inhaled.

Lyria stepped forward. Kaelis caught her arm. "Lyr..."

Lyria turned, meeting her eyes. Resolved.

The rim of the Well fell away in a smooth, terrible curve, stone peeling back like a held breath finally released. Wind surged upward, warm, ancient, snapping wings wide as gravity reversed itself.

Lyria cried out as the world dropped from beneath her. Kaelis grabbed her wrist without looking, the two of them pulled forward together as Zeynar lunged, tail wrapping once around the edge before it vanished beneath his grip. Fizzlewing yelped, a streak of gold, as he shot downward after them.

For a single suspended heartbeat, they were weightless.

Then they were falling.

Down through mist and echo, through air that remembered wings, through a vast hollow that did not close around them, but welcomed. Sound unraveled as light thinned. Then stone met their feet with a low, resonant hum, as though the Well itself had decided where they belonged. Lyria staggered once, then steadied, breath sharp in her chest as the mark at her neck cooled from fire to warmth.

For a heartbeat, no one moved.

Eldrin turned. He had been standing near the inner curve of the chamber, dagger lowered but ready, the light at its edge steady and watchful. His gaze snapped to Lyria and held. Relief crossed his face too quickly to stop. "Lyria," he breathed.

She nodded once.

Gantar exhaled softly, tension easing from his shoulders as he took in the full group, Kaelis braced and feral at Lyria's side, Zeynar alert but controlled, Fizzlewing hovering with uncharacteristic restraint. "You made it," the old sage said quietly.

Thalendir stepped forward a pace, eyes flicking from Eldrin to Lyria, then to the spiraling clouds far above.

Aelar did not speak. His hand remained near his blade, gaze fixed upward, jaw set as if he already sensed what was coming.

The Well opened around them in vast, curving tiers of stone, worn smooth not by feet, but by wings. The air here was still, holding sound without ever giving it back. Far above, clouds continued their endless spiral inward.

Fizzlewing hovered lower, glow dimming. "Oh," he murmured. "That's... not good."

Lyria felt it first. The mark at her neck pulsed once. Not hot, or painful. Aware.

Eldrin's hand went to his side without conscious thought. The Aetherstone warmed beneath his fingers, like something long asleep drawing its first full breath. At the same moment, the dagger at his hip answered, its edge catching light that did not come from above or below, but from within the stone itself.

Gantar inhaled sharply. The pendant at his throat had begun to glow. He closed his eyes.

"Do you hear it?" Finnian asked quietly, one hand rising toward his temples. The marks there shimmered, not flaring, not screaming, but tuning, as though something had finally found the correct pitch.

Thalendir's brow furrowed. "I don't hear anything."

"That's because it's not sound," Gantar said, voice low. "It's memory."

Stone beneath their feet thrummed, not vibrating so much as agreeing, a low resonance that traveled upward through bone and breath alike. The spiraling clouds above them slowed, just slightly, as if listening.

Eldrin swallowed as something pressed against his chest in recognition. His breath caught, then steadied. A shape his lungs remembered. A memory. One his mother had taught him. The sound that left him was not a word. It was a single, low note, rough, untrained, pulled from somewhere beneath language itself.

The Well stilled as every artifact answered at once. His dagger brightened as the Aetherstone flared with warmth sharpening into clarity. Gantar's pendant responded in harmony.

Far above them, something ancient turned its head.

And Eldrin understood, with a certainty that made his hands tremble, this was what he had carried for so long. Deep in his soul. Afraid to release it.

For a heartbeat, no one moved.

Eldrin lifted his head, startled, not by sound, but by absence. As though the world had leaned closer, listening. A song filled his chest. One that had waited since the world first broke.

And this time, he did not resist it.

The sound left him without force. Without volume or demand. It moved outward like breath released after holding too long, threading through stone and sky, through memory and marrow, carrying with it the truth of what had been lost... and what still might be chosen.

The Cry of Dragons had been released, and it was too late to stop it.

"What was that?" Kaelis asked.

Eldrin swayed, one hand against his side, breath coming shallow. "I don't..." He shook his head. "I didn't mean to."

The Well was silent again. Too silent. As the realms decided.

Above the Well, the clouds shifted. Not parting, but thickening. A low wind stirred the ashless stone, carrying with it a scent that did not belong to victory, metal and smoke and something old and hungry. From the far edges of the sky, shadows began to move, slow, deliberate, answering.

Chapter 23

Drakor felt it first. Before he heard it. Before the dragon below the earth moved. Before the world could respond.

Deep within the Dragon Graveyard, the place where life and death had mingled once before, a heartbeat echoed. A resonance older than the realms themselves.

Scales shifted against ancient bone. A breath, ragged, resurrected, trembled through the vast hollows, as if the mountain exhaled. The buried chambers shivered as a low rumble rolled through them, like the first growl of a storm long held at bay. Old magic unfurled, spilling through cracks in stone, threading into the wind, racing across the distances between the realms.

From the depths, a cry rose, haunting. Howling. Alive.

A sound born of death and rebirth, a dragon's call that split the silence of the Graveyard. Stone scraped as claws flexed and scales lifted in a shuddering ripple. And in the darkness, a single emerald eye blazed open.

Zyressa.

A shockwave surged across the land as the prophecy inhaled its next breath.

The earth trembled with a resonance older than dragons themselves, a vibration not only in stone and soil, but in the unseen realms.

The sound rose again, carrying force as its echo spread across the world. The Cry of Dragons was no longer memory. It was alive.

Zyressa's breath hitched as air tore into her lungs. The sky darkened, shadows bent inward as the air thinned, stretched taut by a presence it had been waiting for. She snarled, jaws snapping as claws tore at the earth around her.

Drakor felt it then, fully, unmistakably. He was too late to stop it. Too weak to challenge it. And so he did not resist.

His wings tightened against his scarred sides as he turned toward her, not with ceremony, not with loyalty, but with decision. If darkness was going to resurrect, it would do so on his terms. And when the world burned, it would remember who opened the door.

Drakor dug his claws into the stone, ripping away ash and soil buried beneath centuries of bone and silence. Dust and fragments sprayed into the air as the ground yielded.

Rain began to fall. It came steady and cold, soaking into soil that did not drink it, weighing down wings, dulling color, muting sound. Shadows lengthened where no shadow should have reached, pooling beneath trees, clinging to ravines, crawling along the edges of things that once held firm.

Across the land, fires guttered. Torches burned lower. Ancient wards flickered, not failing, but remembering fear. Wyverns screamed into the sky as nemods surged forward and dark elves broke cover as they circled the Well.

Drakor's lips curled, baring scarred fangs in something almost like a smile. "Let her rise as they gather," he said softly. "It will make the taking easier."

And when the time came, he would use them, use everything, to take what was owed.

Chapter 24

The song stirred through Eldrin a second time, as though calling to dragons once, wasn't enough. Gantar's gaze lifted slowly, tracking the spiraling clouds far above. His mouth pressed into a thin line.

Finnian swallowed, fingers brushing his temples. The silver light there had dimmed, but not vanished. "They heard it," he said. "Didn't they?"

"Yes," Gantar replied. "Everything that remembers did."

Thalendir's hand tightened on his sword. "Then they'll come."

"They're already here," Aelar said quietly, looking up where shadows crossed the cloud cover.

Eldrin straightened slowly, the Aetherstone burning now, not hot, not wild, but heavy, as though it had settled into its true weight at last. "I didn't choose this," he said hoarsely.

Gantar looked at him then. "No," the sage said. "But you remembered. Because the heart was made to carry it."

The air thickened, as though the hollow beneath them were deciding what it would allow to pass through it.

"You mean I was supposed to do that?" Eldrin asked, turning to Gantar.

The stone beneath their feet answered with a low, resonant hum, as if it were listening.

Gantar's voice was quiet. Certain. "Yes," he said.

Eldrin felt the Aetherstone warm at his side. And then, too late to be coincidence, something answered back from within the Well.

Gantar's breath caught. His hand rose instinctively to the fragment at his chest, fingers curling as warmth bled through metal and into bone alike. His eyes widened, in recognition so sharp it bordered on grief. "It was never missing," he whispered. "It's here."

"What's here?" Eldrin asked.

"The third piece," said Gantar as he met Eldrin's gaze. "Of the Aetherstone."

The Well shifted in uneasy layers, and far above, where sky met claw and shadow, the hunt had found its direction.

Wyvern wings cut against the thinning clouds, banking wide arcs that circled but never crossed the inner ring. Dark forms gathered along the upper tiers, bows drawn but not loosed, blades glinting in patient silence. Even the nemods clung to the stone's edge rather than breach it, their half-formed bodies rippling as though something older than command held them back.

They had found the Well. But they were waiting.

Not for weakness.

For arrival.

Chapter 25

The earth gave way with a sound like breath released after holding it too long. Stone cracked, not violently, not all at once, but with a slow, reverent surrender, as if the grave itself had finally decided to remember what it had buried. Ash slid inward. Bone shifted. The vast basin of the Dragon Graveyard trembled beneath Drakor's talons as the ground beneath him opened further.

He worked with patience born of survival, claws digging, levering slabs of stone aside, tearing through layers of sediment and calcified scale. Each movement sent dull echoes through the graveyard, stirring dust that had not risen since the last dragon had fallen screaming into silence.

Below him, something moved. Zyressa's breath came ragged and uneven, dragging air into lungs that had forgotten how to rise. The sound scraped against the hollow chambers beneath the earth, wet, painful, but alive.

Drakor paused. For the first time since the Cry had torn through the world, he did not smile. She lay half-entombed beneath the remains of others, ribs of ancient dragons collapsed across her flanks, fractured wings draped over her back like a shroud. Emerald scales began to gleam faintly as old magic stirred beneath them.

Zyressa shuddered. Her claws flexed weakly against stone. Her tail twitched, dislodging fragments of bone that clattered down into the dark. A low, broken sound tore from her throat, not a roar, but a protest against death.

Drakor stepped closer. "You hear it now," he murmured. "The world calling you back."

Zyressa's head shifted, heavy and unsteady. One eye cracked open, emerald, blazing even through the haze of resurrection. It fixed on him at once. Recognition sparked first. Then fury. Her jaw snapped weakly, teeth scraping stone inches from his talons. Fire sputtered uselessly in her chest, smoke leaking from her nostrils in short, furious bursts.

Drakor did not retreat. "We must rise together," he said softly. "Before it's too late."

Her wings convulsed, scraping against the bones pinning them down. The graveyard answered with a low groan, stone and remains shifting as if uneasy with what it was returning to the world.

Zyressa growled, deeper this time. The sound rolled through the basin and did not fade.

Drakor felt it then. "You were never meant to stay buried," he continued, circling her slowly, careful to remain just beyond the reach of her claws. "This place is full of endings. But you..." His gaze flicked to the faint shimmer beginning to gather along her scales. "...you were not meant for death."

The air above them changed as the sky darkened, as if something unseen leaned closer, curious.

Zyressa's breath hitched again. Her chest heaved, scales along her ribs lifting and falling as old magic surged unevenly through her body. She snarled, fire flaring briefly in her throat, this time hot enough to scorch stone.

Drakor smiled then. Thin. Sharp. He lowered his head slightly, close enough that she could hear. "Darkness is calling us."

The ground beneath Zyressa's chest began to glow with pattern. Lines emerged beneath her scales, ancient, deliberate, threading outward from her heart in slow, inevitable paths. The magic did not rush or blaze. It burned.

Zyressa screamed. The sound tore free of her chest in a violent surge, raw, furious, alive. It shattered the stillness of the graveyard, echoing across bone and stone and memory itself.

Drakor staggered back a single step as power rolled outward. Emerald light bled along Zyressa's chest, settling into a symbol older than any realm, a convergence of lines and curves as it was branded into her scales.

The third mark. **The final echo of the prophecy made flesh.**

She convulsed once more, then her breathing evened. She flexed her wings, strong now, tearing free of the bones that had bound them. Ancient remains shattered beneath the force, collapsing inward as she rose, dragging herself fully from the earth.

Drakor watched as the graveyard bowed.

Because darkness had answered the Cry and with it, the balance had tipped.

Drakor felt the weakening before the chains snapped.

Far beneath them, far deeper than the graveyard, deeper than memory itself, the ancient wards shuddered, stretched thin by weight they had never been meant to withstand. Undone by the scale tipping.

The sky split with dark intent, clouds twisting into vast, impossible shapes. Across the realms, ancient signals ignited, marks burned, wards faltered, bindings long trusted cracked under the strain.

And somewhere in the Abyss, something laughed.

The rupture tore wider. A presence surged upward, vast, incandescent with rage held too long in check. Fury poured through the broken seals like breath drawn after drowning, violent, disorienting, alive.

The air screamed as ancient weight reclaimed motion, memory slamming back into form.

Vartharax rose. Not cleanly, or wholly as earth resisted him.

Stone split in grinding layers as claws forced upward through burial that had never been meant to break. Packed soil and shattered bone collapsed around him as he tore through the dead weight of centuries, dragging himself through darkness that clung, that pressed, that tried to hold.

It failed.

The Cry had reached him. Not as sound—but as rupture. A tearing of alignment. A shift in the balance that had once bound him beneath the world. The light that held him did not break. It tilted.

And that was enough.

The ground convulsed as he surged higher, wings forcing space where none existed, scales grinding against stone as the abyss gave way inch by inch.

The world had buried him. The world had chosen to forget him.

But it had never unmade him.

And now, it remembered.

He felt the marks burn across the world—two that had held, anchoring light against him—and the third. Dark. Now awakened. On one of his kind.

His wings drove downward. Stone shattered, and the world gave way beneath him.

The ground split wide as the force of his ascent tore him free of the abyss, earth collapsing in his wake as he surged upward through layers that had once buried him. Air rushed to meet him, thin, then tearing, as his full weight forced space where none remained.

The sky screamed as something immense tore through it, clouds collapsing inward as shadow claimed motion and will was returned to flesh. Vartharax turned without hesitation. Toward the convergence. Toward the place where memory, mark, and shadows now collided.

Far below, wings faltered. Creatures that had never known fear felt it anyway, an instinct older than thought, older than command. The air itself seemed to recoil ahead of him, thinning as though the sky could not bear his passing.

The dark lord was coming. And the Well of Wings waited…

Chapter 26

Vartharax circled. High above the Well, his vast wings carved slow, deliberate arcs through the collapsing sky, each pass tightening the spiral of cloud and shadow beneath him. He did not rush. He measured, and listened.

Below, the hollow waited. The marks burned, and the stone remembered.

His head tilted slightly, as though tasting the shape of the moment, of power gathered, of resistance aligned against him.

And then, he chose.

Stone groaned, not splitting, not collapsing, but yielding, as though something vast had leaned its weight against the world from the other side. The air thickened, pulling inward toward a point above the hollow, clouds spiraling down as if drawn by a gravity that did not belong to sky. A pressure rolled across the rim.

Wyverns faltered mid-arc, banking wide to clear the space above the inner ring. Dark elves lowered their blades, not in retreat, but in instinctive deference. Even the nemods flattened against the stone, their forms shuddering as though answering a summons older than their making.

The sky did not open. It was displaced.

Wings vast as a mountain cut through the storm and dropped past the gathered forces at impossible speed. Shadow spilled over the rim, stretching too far, bending where it should not bend. Light did not vanish. It recoiled.

The dark ranks held at the edge, forming a widening ring of absence. The space below belonged to him alone.

And Vartharax descended.

He struck the Well like a verdict. Stone rippled outward beneath the impact, dust lifting in a slow ring that hung suspended between heartbeats. Black wings unfurled, measured and absolute. Even the echoes died.

Vartharax lifted his massive head, and his gaze swept the chamber. It passed over the gathered figures within the inner ring, over wings half-raised, blades held but not yet swung, faces turned toward him in defiance or dread. It skimmed the carved walls of the Well, the spiraled names pressed into stone, the fracture Gantar had not yet opened. He took it in as though it were already his.

Then his eyes fixed on Eldrin. The weight of that attention struck harder than any blow, and Silverwind trembled, hooves skidding as if the stone itself had turned uncertain.

The Aetherstone flared at Eldrin's side, burning with recognition as the dagger answered in a steady, unyielding glow.

And when the dark lord spoke, the sound filled the chamber.

"So," Vartharax said, amusement curling through the sound like smoke through flame, "the song has found its way back."

Eldrin dropped forward in the saddle as the Aetherstone at his side flared white-hot, pain and recognition lancing through him at once. His fingers clenched against Silverwind's mane as the dagger at his hip answered in kind.

"Eldrin!" Finnian shouted, reaching for him, silver light flaring instinctively at his temples, then stalling, smothered beneath the sheer weight pressing down on the Well.

Gantar moved his horse forward a step, then stopped.

The dark lord's eyes burned like embers. Smoke rolled over his maw as his tongue tasted the air. His presence shifted, subtle, almost curious, toward Eldrin, who stood before him.

Then a laugh rolled across the space, low and terrible, felt more than heard. "Well," the dragon lord said, his voice curling with dark amusement, "you are not what I expected."

His vast head tilted, just slightly. Heat rolled as his gaze narrowed, not in threat, but in assessment. The air between them thickened, as if Vartharax were tasting something unfamiliar and finding it... interesting.

Thalendir's hand tightened on his sword. Kaelis shifted closer to Lyria, blades half-raised, and Zeynar's wings flexed, shield angling instinctively. None of it mattered because Vartharax had already chosen his focus.

Eldrin forced himself upright and did not look away. "But you," he said, "are exactly what I expected."

The words surprised even him. But they rang true.

Vartharax's eyes burned brighter, embers flaring as memory stirred. A slow, terrible smile curved along the dragon's maw. "Ah," he murmured. "I see it now..."

"Tell me, Prince," Vartharax said softly, almost indulgently, "did they ever tell you the truth?"

The words slid across the Well like oil over water, and the silence shattered.

Eldrin's grip tightened on his blade. "What truth?" he asked.

Vartharax drifted closer, massive limbs moving with unsettling ease, circling, not in haste, not in threat, but with the patience of something that had already decided its prey.

"No," the dragon lord murmured, a smirk tugged at his maw... "Of course they didn't."

He tilted his head, studying Eldrin as one might examine a fracture in stone. "Do you know what breaks a world, prince?" he asked.

"It is not darkness or war," He said. "It is convincing the innocent that exile is mercy."

Eldrin's breath caught. He turned to the sage. "What's he talking about, Gantar?"

Gantar did not answer. Instead, his gaze lifted, not to Vartharax, but to the carvings spiraling up the Well's inner walls. Names. Wings. Fractured histories pressed into stone. The silence pressed in, thick and expectant.

"It was a long time ago," Gantar said at last.

"Ask him how the Covenant broke," the dark lord said as a low rumble rolled from his chest.

Gantar's hand tightened around the pendant at his throat as his eyes met Eldrin's.

Vartharax's lips curled, smoke leaking between blackened teeth. "He deserves to know," the dark lord murmured. "Doesn't he?"

The Well stirred again, stone warming, light threading faintly through the carvings above them.

Eldrin's chest felt too tight. "Know what?" he asked.

Gantar closed his eyes. Just for a moment.

"Still skirting the truth," the dark lord murmured. "How very elven of you."

"No," Gantar said. "But some truths do not need to be inherited."

Vartharax's gaze returned to Eldrin, heavy with something like satisfaction. He tasted the air and found another victim.

His head turned toward Thalendir. "You were old enough to remember," Vartharax said, his massive head lowered until his eyes were level with him. "When she was cast out."

Thalendir's grip tightened on his sword until the leather creaked. "I don't..." he began, then stopped. His breath hitched, shallow and sharp. He shook his head once, as if to dislodge the memory before it could take shape.

Vartharax watched him with open interest now. "Did they tell you why she was sent away?"

For a heartbeat, everything else faded for Thalendir, even the low hum of the Well itself, replaced by something thin and distant. A corridor half-remembered. Stone cool beneath bare feet. Laughter, quick, bright, with gold hair and blue eyes.

"She did not choose exile," Vartharax said quietly. "She was chosen for it."

Stone groaned beneath his slow, circling steps.

"When they learned what she carried," Vartharax added softly, "it was not enemies that condemned her."

His vast shadow passed over them like a closing door.

"Those who loved her gave her up."

Thalendir's breath stuttered. "No."

"Oh yes," Vartharax replied gently. "Not the council. Not the priests. Not the crowd who later learned to hate what they had been taught to fear." His eyes flared, brief, vicious. "Your father."

The word struck harder than any blow.

Vartharax's voice dropped, intimate as confession. "I whispered fear," he admitted. "I sharpened doubt. I showed him what might be lost."

A breath of smoke curled between them.

"But I did not make the choice."

His eyes burned as they fixed on Thalendir. "The crown weighed heavy," Vartharax continued. "The realm trembled. And when presented with a choice between love and order..." He tilted his head.

"...he chose order."

Thalendir's jaw clenched. "You lie."

"Do I?" Vartharax said. "Or were you simply taught to forget?"

Thalendir swallowed. Images aligned, not memory, not vision, but truth pressing through old stone. An elven king beneath banners that did not bend. An elf standing alone, wings folded tight against herself. A door closing.

The Well warmed again, stone beneath their feet humming faintly, insistently.

Thalendir's sword dipped.

Gantar inhaled sharply. "Enough," he said.

But the damage was already done.

"Tell me who he's talking about," said Eldrin.

Thalendir turned to his brother. Something raw and unguarded flickered across his face. Confusion. Anger. Grief whose name he'd forgotten.

A pause.

"It was before you were born," he said hoarsely.

Eldrin shook his head, throat tight. "Who was she?"

Thalendir looked his brother in the eye and swallowed.

"Our sister."

The words did not make sense. They slid past Eldrin's understanding, struck something deeper, and stopped there, lodged like a blade that refused to be pulled free.

"Sister?" Eldrin repeated quietly.

The Well seemed to tilt. His chest tightened, breath shallow and unsteady. The Aetherstone burned against his side, not flaring, not warning, mourning.

"How can that be..." Eldrin stopped. He looked to Gantar, but the sage did not look back. Something cold settled in Eldrin's gut as the truth took shape, not fully, not yet, but enough to hurt.

Vartharax's low chuckle rolled through the Well.

"Go ahead..." he murmured. "Tell him about Thalyndra."

The name struck like a blade between the ribs, and Thalendir went still.

Gantar did not look at him or Eldrin.

The dragon's gaze sharpened, fixing them in place. "When they learned what she carried," he added, "fear hardened their hearts."

"They told her it was for the realm," Vartharax went on. "That her leaving would preserve peace. That love, her love, was too dangerous to keep." His wings flexed, shadows folding inward.

Eldrin's breath came shallow as he turned to the sage. "What did she carry?"

Gantar's voice was quiet when he answered. "Life."

Silence cracked.

"The first drelf," Vartharax said, savoring the fracture.

"Mine."

Thalendir staggered back a step as years of hatred collapsed inward, doctrine turning on itself, a war aimed at his own blood and never known.

"They did not call it cruelty," Vartharax went on. "They called it... mercy."

His gaze burned as it fixed on Thalendir. "And when your father was forced to choose between love and order..."

A pause.

"...he chose order."

The Well hummed, low and insistent, as if sealing the truth into stone.

Vartharax straightened at last, wings spreading just enough to blot the light. "So now," he said, voice deepening, "tell me, princes..."

A smile like a wound.

"Will you defend the choice that broke your bloodline?"

Chapter 27

Eldrin did not look at the dragon. He looked at Gantar. "Is it true?" he asked. The words came out steadier than he felt.

For a long moment, the sage did not answer. The hum of the Well pressed in around them.

"Yes," Gantar said at last. "It is."

Vartharax inhaled deeply, savoring the fracture he had just widened.

"And now," the dragon lord said, wings spreading wider, shadows pooling beneath them, "the sons stand together at the place where it began. How convenient."

His gaze swept from Thalendir to Eldrin.

"I broke the Covenant," Vartharax said calmly. "I deceived your sister."

His gaze sharpened. "And when your mother followed me here with blade in hand... she failed."

Eldrin moved the moment Vartharax spoke of his mother. Something snapped clean through him. "No," he said, voice sharp, raw. He pulled Silverwind forward half a step before he realized he'd moved at all. The dagger at his side flared, blue light cutting through the bruised air like a wound reopening.

"You don't get to speak of her," he said. "Not you."

Vartharax's gaze locked on his. Ah.

Recognition bloomed.

"So," the dragon murmured, his eyes lit. "The blade has learned who forged it."

Heat surged through Eldrin's chest as he spoke. "My mother did not fail. She..."

"She loved," Vartharax interrupted smoothly. "That was her flaw."

Eldrin moved Silverwind forward again, fire in his eyes.

The dark lord narrowed his brow. His tail switched from side to side, carving shallow furrows in the stone as if the ground itself were something he might test for weakness. The corners of his mouth curved upward. "You..." he said, eyes burning into Eldrin. "Think you can defeat darkness?"

Vartharax pressed forward, no longer curious or amused.

The dark fire inside his maw did not strike like flame. It weighted the air, forcing Silverwind back step by measured step, each hoof scraping against stone as though the Well itself were counting.

The Aetherstone burned against Eldrin's side. Its light pulsed, slower now, heavier, like breath drawn through failing lungs. The dagger at his hip throbbed in answer.

"You carry what does not belong to you," the dragon said, voice tightening as he advanced.

Eldrin did not answer. He moved.

Silverwind surged forward as his heels struck her sides. Stone blurred beneath them. Eldrin drew the dagger in one fluid motion, and its light tore free, bright, defiant, as he drove straight for the dragon's throat.

For a heartbeat, it looked possible.

Vartharax did not step aside. His tail moved. Not fast, but certain. The strike came like a collapsing wall. Scaled muscle slammed into Silverwind's chest, and the world tore loose beneath Eldrin.

The impact ripped him from the saddle as horse and rider were flung apart. Stone rushed up hard and fast. Eldrin hit shoulder-first and rolled, breath exploding from his lungs as momentum hurled him across the inner curve of the Well. Armor shrieked against stone as he skidded and slammed to a halt in a spray of dust. The dagger tore free from his grasp. It spun once through the air, silver fire flickering, and struck the stone with a hollow crack, skittering away into the gloom.

For a moment the world rang with silence.

Silverwind staggered first. Blood streaked her flank, but she forced herself upright, shaking, trembling, yet unbroken.

Eldrin dragged air into his lungs like broken glass and pushed himself onto one knee.

Vartharax advanced. "So eager," the dragon murmured. "So predictable."

Darkness gathered in his chest, dense, coiling. The breath before fire.

"ELDRIN..." Finnian shouted.

Gantar stepped forward and planted his staff hard against the stone. The crack rang through the Well like struck metal. Stone split outward beneath the impact, not breaking, but opening, as the pendant at Gantar's chest flared white and blinding. Light answered from below.

Vartharax's smile faltered. His head turned slowly toward the sage, vast body coiling as ancient certainty slipped beneath his claws. His gaze dropped to the light burning at the sage's chest.

"That stone," the dark lord hissed, eyes locking onto Gantar, "should have burned your heart hollow."

Gantar lifted his gaze. "It did," he replied. "And it taught me."

The dragon's wings flexed, stone groaning beneath their weight. Shadows crawled outward from his talons, reaching toward Gantar like grasping fingers. "You mistake knowledge for strength," Vartharax growled as his gaze burned into the sage. "You cannot defeat me..."

"No," Gantar said, voice steady even as the air screamed around him. "But I know what can."

His hand closed around the Aetherstone fragment at his chest as he stepped fully into the Well's inner ring.

A low hum rose through the stone, resonant and ancient, threading through the air, like a name spoken after centuries of silence.

Gantar's breath caught. "I am here to *return what was taken*."

"You dare…" The dragon lunged and air folded inward as Vartharax struck, his head snapped forward, pressure slamming into the space where Gantar stood. Stone cracked outward in a widening ring. The Well groaned as if bracing itself.

Gantar did not move aside. He stepped into it. His staff struck the stone once, hard, and light answered. Not outward.

Down.

The Aetherstone at his chest flared white-hot as he lifted his free hand, fingers splayed, and the pressure broke against him; not stopped, not defeated, but *held*. For a heartbeat, the force of the dragon's will shuddered and split around him, diverted into the stone itself.

The Well reacted. A deep resonance rose from below, threading through Gantar's bones, through the staff, through the fragment burning at his chest.

Vartharax recoiled a fraction. "Give me the stone—" he hissed.

Gantar's knees trembled as the light intensified. Pain carved through him, not sharp, but vast, as though something bound to his very life was being pulled free. He did not resist it.

Deep within the Well, something awakened as it rose to meet him, and resonance aligned.

Vartharax's fire collapsed inward, dragged toward the opening heart of the Well. But it did not yield. The dark lord roared, forcing the collapse to stall, his will slamming back against the pull of the stone. Flame twisted, resisting, warping into something heavier, denser, as though he would crush the Well itself before surrendering to it.

"No," he snarled, voice splitting the air.

The pressure surged, and the light around Gantar shuddered, bending under the force as the dragon's power pressed inward, seeking to break him, to scatter the fragile alignment before it could complete.

Gantar staggered. His knees dipped, but he did not fall. His hand tightened around the burning fragment at his chest as the light flared brighter, blinding now, no longer contained, no longer gentle. The resonance deepened, pulling harder, drawing not just from the stone, but from him.

"It belongs here," Gantar whispered.

The Stone answered, but not to Vartharax.

Gantar's grip faltered, his knees gave. The staff splintered in his hands as he dropped forward, the light passing through him, not around him, not from him, but through.

The pendant at his chest dissolved into radiance, threads of white fire tearing free and falling toward the center of the hollow. For a moment, Gantar held there. Not breaking. Releasing. Then the strength left him.

When the light faded, the Aetherstone lay at the heart of the Well. The ground shifted.

And Gantar smiled.

Chapter 28

Eldrin felt it as soon as Gantar's staff broke. Not as light, as absence. The weight at his side tore free in a sudden surge of heat. The fragment of the Aetherstone ripped loose from its binding and shot from his belt in a streak of white fire, drawn toward the awakened heart of the Well. Stone struck stone below.

Alignment.

The Well answered with a deep pulse that rolled through the chamber like a heartbeat returned. The Aetherstone was whole.

The dagger ignited in answer. Eldrin surged to his feet, seized the blade from the ground, and swung into Silverwind's saddle in a single motion.

This time the fire did not press him back. The Well pulsed beneath the mare's hooves, steady and deep, as though marking the cost already paid.

Vartharax drew breath again. Angrier now. And for the first time, uncertain.

"What have you DONE?" the dark lord thundered. Fire collapsed inward as the Well drank it down, breaking the dragon's dominion into something the ancient stone no longer obeyed.

Eldrin did not hesitate. He rode straight through the thinning fire, blue light clean and steady in his grasp. He leaned low over Silverwind's neck, dagger raised, heart hammering so hard it felt as though it might tear free of his chest.

Silverwind leapt. Blue light wrapped his arm, his chest, his breath, cool where it touched, steady where the fire tried to crush him.

As he struck, the Well did not resist.

And this time, the blade did not falter.

Vartharax screamed. The dagger buried to the hilt, light flooding outward from the wound as though the blade had pierced not flesh, but the lie holding him together.

The fire in his chest folded inward, devouring its own heat. "No..." the dragon thundered, wings beating, sending shockwaves across the Well.

Eldrin held fast. "You are finished," he said, voice steady as stone.

Light surged upward from the Well's heart. It poured through the fracture Gantar had opened, through the place where memory had been torn apart, threading through the blade, the marks, the Stone.

Vartharax reared back as the shadow around him began to tear free, sloughing away in strips like smoke unraveling in a rising wind. "This world..." he rasped, voice breaking into echoes that no longer aligned with his body. "Will..."

Eldrin did not withdraw the blade. He leaned in. "Forget your name," he said.

The dagger flared once, brilliant, clean, final.

Vartharax's roar cut off mid-breath. His vast form collapsed inward, shadow imploding into itself as if the Well had inhaled him whole. Wings disintegrated into smoke. Scales fractured into lightless dust. Fire guttered, then vanished.

What remained did not fall. It dissolved. Ash spiraled upward, caught in a wind that no longer carried malice, only release. The pressure crushing the Well vanished in an instant, leaving silence so complete it rang.

Vartharax was no more.

The dagger dimmed in Eldrin's hand, its glow fading to a steady, living light.

The Well exhaled.

And for the first time since the Covenant broke, the world stood still.

Chapter 29

Eldrin remained where he was, the dagger still in his hand, its glow fading from blinding white to a steady, living silver. His hands trembled from the sudden absence of resistance. As though he had been bracing against a storm that no longer existed.

Silverwind quivered beneath him, her head lowering almost to the stone. The crushing pressure in the air eased, like lungs finally drawing a full breath.

"You..." Finnian swallowed, eyes fixed on Eldrin. "You did it."

Thalendir stared at the empty space where Vartharax had stood, his sword hanging loose in his grip. For the first time since elfhood, his face held no calculation, no judgment, only disbelief. Then he turned, his focus on where the sage fell. "Gantar..." he said as he moved toward the body.

Kaelis lowered her blade. Her wings folded slowly, reverently, as though afraid sudden movement might undo what had been won.

Zeynar sank to one knee, head bowed, not in submission, but in acknowledgment.

The silence stretched.

Eldrin lowered the dagger. The weight of it seemed greater now, as if victory had given it permission to be heavy again. His breath came unevenly, the tremor in his hands climbing into his arms. He looked at the stone. At the place where Gantar lay.

The sage's body was still, silver hair fanned across the dark surface, his face peaceful in a way Eldrin had never seen before, not even in sleep. The lines of strain were gone. The watchfulness stilled.

He had gone willingly. That truth struck harder than the dragon ever had.

Thalendir stooped beside the body. His sword slipped from numb fingers and struck the stone with a hollow sound. He knelt. "He knew," he said, voice rough. "Didn't he?"

Eldrin swallowed. His throat burned. "Yes."

Thalendir bowed his head, not as a prince. Not as a commander. As an elf who had just lost a friend.

Finnian stood a few paces back, hands clenched at his sides. He searched for something light to say, something that might ease the weight, but the words refused to come. The mark at his temples had gone quiet.

Lyria had not moved. Her silver wings folded close, catching the faint glow of the Well. One hand rested over the mark at her neck, fingers splayed as though steadying something fragile inside her.

Eldrin swung down from the saddle. His boots struck stone, the sound too loud in the quiet that followed. Instinctively, his hand went to his side.

And found nothing.

No warmth. No pulse. No steady presence where the Aetherstone had once rested.

The absence hollowed him. He closed his hand into a fist and forced himself to breathe as he crossed the stone. Each step toward Gantar felt heavier than the last, as though the Well itself demanded acknowledgment of what had been paid.

He dropped to his knees and for a long moment, he could not speak. He reached out, fingers brushing Gantar's sleeve, then tightening as though anchoring himself to something solid. "You told me," Eldrin said at last, voice raw. "You told me I wouldn't have to do this alone."

The words broke as they left him.

"I believed you."

His head bowed.

In that moment, he was not the Blade. Not the prince. Not the bearer of prophecy. He was a young elf kneeling beside the one who had stood between him and the dark.

"I didn't ask you to give your life," he whispered. "I would have carried the weight longer. I would have..."

His voice failed. He pressed his forehead to the stone beside Gantar's shoulder, breath hitching, tears falling soundlessly.

Beside him, Thalendir remained still. Watching his brother undone, unguarded, broke something old and rigid inside him. "He chose," Thalendir said quietly.

Finnian turned away, granting Eldrin the dignity of grief. Kaelis stood with her wings folded in reverence.

And the Well, which had once borne witness to betrayal, now bore witness to sacrifice.

Chapter 30

And Lyria—Lyria felt it then. Not as memory, but as presence.

Eldrin's grief struck her like a breaking wave—raw, unguarded, achingly familiar. It collided with something deep in her chest, a resonance she had carried since the moment the Tree Sage tore her past from her mind. Warmth bloomed there, as though something long surrendered was finding its way home—not through magic, but through completion.

The hollow she had learned to ignore shifted—not empty now, but waiting. Tears slipped down her face, unashamed.

Across the stone, Eldrin lifted his head, and as their eyes met, the world realigned.

Beneath their feet, the Well answered—not with light, but with harmony. A low resonance spread through the stone, deep and steady, as though something long fractured had remembered its shape.

Lyria gasped. The warmth in her chest flared—not sharp, not blinding, but whole. And the gates did not open gently. They fell.

She saw Eldrin in the forest, standing between her and death as nemods closed in. She felt the impact of his body shielding hers as they tumbled through the Elven portal. His voice steady when everything else broke. His hands refusing to let go, pulling her bleeding body to Gantar's door.

She saw the Vale—the way he never left her side even when she pretended not to need him. Then the dragon graveyard—the way he looked at her right before he fell. The cage of dark elves. His silence. His restraint. His choosing her freedom over his own longing.

The truth did not return in fragments. It returned all at once.

Her knees buckled as it crashed through her, breath tearing from her in a sob she could not contain.

"Eldrin—"

His name left her like an oath.

She crossed the stone without thinking. Her hands found him as though they had never forgotten the shape of his face.

"I remember," she said, voice shaking. "I remember everything."

Eldrin stilled. For a heartbeat he did not move, as though afraid that reaching for her might shatter what had just been restored.

Then he pulled her into him.

Her wings flared as his arms closed around her. Forehead to forehead. Breath to breath.

And something rose through the Well.

Not power.

Not command.

Recognition.

Chapter 31

The graveyard did not tremble. It inhaled.

Drakor felt it before he understood it, a sudden, violent absence where pressure had once lived. The thread that had bound his will to another snapped cleanly. The sky shifted, not in sound, but in silence, as far beyond stone and bone, something immense had ended.

Drakor froze. His head snapped toward the distant horizon, toward the direction of the Well. The connection that had once pulsed like a second heartbeat inside his chest was gone.

A laugh tore from his throat, harsh, jagged, disbelieving. "So," Drakor hissed, scars along his twisted frame pulling tight. "You finally fell."

Relief flooded him. Then exhilaration.

All his life, he had lived beneath another's shadow. Now the weight was gone, and the world lay open before him like prey. The throne was empty.

And he was still standing.

Behind him, Zyressa rose fully from the shattered remains of her kin. Emerald light pulsed once across her chest, the mark blazing against her scales. Alive.

Drakor turned slowly to look at her. The graveyard had bowed. But not to him. The Cry had broken the old order, and the Well had answered. The dark lord had fallen. Now the prophecy had shifted again. The marks were awakened. One for each realm.

"They will look for a master," he growled, eyes burning as he turned fully toward the Well where the mark-bearers were gathered. His gaze sharpened, hunger eclipsing caution. Two burned in the Well, and one now blazed before him. He snarled. "How convenient."

His breath left him in a slow, measured exhale as Zyressa flexed her newly freed wings, scattering ancient bone into dust.

Her gaze snapped to him, no confusion now, no weakness. Awareness sharpened behind those emerald eyes. Not subservience. Calculation.

Above the distant Well, the wyverns waited as the nemods clung to stone and dark elves held their breath. They did not yet know their master was ash.

Drakor's gaze lingered on the symbol etched into Zyressa's scales. A slow smile curved his crooked maw. "The balance has not tipped," he said softly. "It has opened."

And this time, he would not serve.

Zyressa stood in the shattered graveyard, emerald fire burning steady across her chest. Rain hissed against her scales, turning to steam where it struck the mark. The scent of scorched earth and ancient dust rose around her as broken bones slid from her wings and clattered down the slopes of the graves. The Cry still trembled through her bones.

Drakor felt it too, the echo moving outward through sky and stone alike, vibrating through the hollowed ribs of long-dead dragons beneath his talons. "The dark lord is gone," he said.

Her gaze snapped to him, pupils narrowing to slits. "I felt it," he continued. "His dominion... unraveled."

Thunder rolled across the mountains. Far beyond the graveyard, clouds twisted inward, rain falling in torrents that streaked the broken spires of stone.

Her mark pulsed once and steadied. "The Cry freed him," she said slowly. "And ended him."

Drakor's jaw tightened. "And it called you."

Her eyes sharpened. "It called dragonkind."

The words seemed to deepen the air between them.

A tremor moved through the ground, not collapse, but awakening. Distant ridgelines shuddered as though something far older than Zyressa had shifted in its sleep.

Drakor stepped closer, lowering his voice though no one stood near enough to overhear. "The marked ones have fled to the Well. My forces circle it. The dark elves have converged. They wait."

"For Vartharax," she said.

"For command," he corrected.

Rain ran in dark lines along his crooked body, tracing old scars. A long silence stretched between them, broken only by thunder and the distant roll of stone unsettled by the Cry's passing.

"If we do not command them and claim the marks," Drakor continued quietly, "they will fracture." He let the next words settle. "And something else will answer."

Zyressa's wings flexed, scattering bone shards down the slope. The mark flared brighter, not in anger. In awareness. "You fear what else the Cry may stir," she said.

Drakor did not look away. "I fear what arrives second," he replied.

Lightning split the sky in the far distance, too far to illuminate clearly, but enough to reveal motion in the storm banks. Shapes, vast and indistinct. "They will come," Drakor added. "All of them."

Her claws dug into the shattered stone, crushing ribs that had once belonged to dragons who had knelt to no one. "You have a plan?" she asked.

Drakor's smile was slight. Calculated. "If you rise before the Cry settles," he said, "they will kneel to you."

The wind shifted, and far above, the sky moved.

Zyressa lifted her head, rain sliding from her jaw in rivulets of silver. "Then we move," she said. "Before the others arrive."

Her wings unfurled fully, vast, scarred, magnificent, scattering grave dust into spirals around her.

Drakor inclined his head, and this time, he did not bother hiding the hunger in his eyes. They launched skyward together, the graveyard trembling as ancient bones collapsed inward beneath the force of their ascent. Storm clouds split around them as they climbed.

And somewhere far beyond sight, beyond mountain, beyond sea, beyond memory, the Cry went unanswered.

For now.

Chapter 32

The storm broke before they did. Clouds convulsed above the Well of Wings, torn apart by the force of something rising through them. Thunder rolled like a drumbeat the sky could not silence.

The wyverns felt it first. Their circling pattern shattered as pressure rippled outward from the approaching dark. Wings faltered mid-beat. Screeches split the air as they banked hard, claws scraping sparks from stone while they fought for position, forming a widening spiral over the hollow.

The dark elves along the upper tiers braced as blades slid free in disciplined unison, metal whispering against leather. A battle horn sounded, low and sustained, its note bending beneath the weight pressing down from the sky. Archers shifted stance, boots grinding against wet stone as bows angled downward toward the enemy.

And nemods answered. They recoiled in their half-formed bodies and writhed atop their mounts, bone blades flexing and reforming as shadow thickened above them. A guttural chorus rose from their throats. They could already taste blood. Their mounts stamped and snorted, smoke hissing from flared nostrils as the air grew heavy and metallic.

The sky darkened further as a presence split the clouds. Zyressa emerged in a streak of emerald and stormlight, her wings carving the sky open as she descended. Rain burned away from her scales in hissing vapor. The mark along her chest flared, brilliant, defiant, and the air bent around her like something acknowledging sovereignty.

Drakor followed at her shoulder, smaller but no less terrible, his crooked wings cutting sharp angles through the gale. His eyes never left the Well.

Below them, stone glowed faintly where the Aetherstone rested whole at its heart. Drakor felt its completion and recognized the threat.

Zyressa slowed as she reached the rim, vast wings beating twice, before she hovered over the inner ring. Her shadow swallowed the tiers. Drakor angled higher, scanning the horizon. They were not alone.

Behind them, the storm thickened as shapes moved within it. Distant wings, scales, hunger. Dragons answering the Cry.

Zyressa's gaze locked on the Well's center, on the figures below, on the elf who had slain a dragon, the drelf whose memory had returned, and the stone that had dared to become whole again. Her lips peeled back from her teeth. "Descend," she commanded.

This time, the wyverns did not hesitate. They dove as dark elves moved as one, leaping from the upper tiers, and nemods followed, spilling like ink torn loose from the page.

And the sky emptied its wrath into the Well.

"Form up!" Eldrin barked, already moving, the dagger flaring back to life in his grip as light raced along its edge. Silverwind reared, shrill and defiant, hooves striking sparks from the stone before she lunged forward beneath him.

Thalendir grabbed Steel's reins and swung into the saddle in one easy motion. Sword up. Gaze locked. His resolve settled into something hard and unbreakable. For his mother. For Gantar. For his kingdom.

Aelar moved to his flank, blade angled low, eyes scanning the upper tiers for the first descent.

Lyria staggered, wings flaring wide to steady herself. The mark at her neck burned hot. The memories still surged through her, raw and overwhelming, but instead of breaking her, they steadied her, and she stepped forward into them.

Kaelis was beside her in a rush of motion, blade drawn, tail low and coiled for strike, scanning the shadows where wyverns would fall first.

"Up there!" Finnian shouted, the words tearing out of him as the pressure at his temples spiked, silver light flashing along the marks. "So much for a quiet ending."

Wind roared downward, not a natural current, but a force drawn toward the heart of the Well. It swallowed battle cries and the shriek of wyverns alike, turning sound into distortion. Dust and rain spiraled upward at once, caught between descent and pull. The convergence above fractured as clouds tore, shadow split, and the first of the enemy began to fall.

Steel screamed as it met claw. The first nemod lunged from the wall, blade flashing, his Shadowmane barreling ahead, but it never reached Eldrin. Silverwind surged forward with a furious whinny, hooves striking stone. The dagger was already in his hand, its light flaring brighter as they charged.

"Left!" Finnian shouted.

Eldrin twisted in the saddle and brought the blade down in a clean arc. Light tore through smoke and flesh alike, the nemod unraveling mid-strike as Silverwind streaked past.

Above them, wyverns dove. Kaelis launched upward with a powerful leap, padded feet striking stone as her sword flashed. Her wings snapped wide to drive momentum, sending her straight into the wyvern's path. She slashed through tendon and scale, then spun as her tail whipped out, spines tearing across the creature's chest. It screamed and crashed hard behind her. She landed low and balanced, claws scraping stone, already moving toward the next threat.

Thalendir rode hard, Steel's black hooves pounding the stone. He cut through the advancing dark elves with disciplined fury and steady resolve.

"Hold the line!" Eldrin called, hauling Silverwind around as another wave surged in.

Lyria took to the air. Silver wings beat until she was above them, light flaring from her mark as she drove downward in a controlled dive, scattering nemods like smoke in a gale. She landed hard beside Zeynar, wings snapping closed as she pivoted, breath steady, eyes clear.

Zeynar moved with her. His sword flashed, low and fast, cutting through a nemod's torso as his tail lashed out in the same breath, spines tearing through another before it could strike. He spun, claws scraping stone, and drove forward again, efficient, relentless.

Finnian ducked beneath a sweeping claw and drove both blades up into a wyvern's chest as it skimmed low, rolling clear as it shrieked and spiraled away. "I am really starting to hate flying things!"

And through the chaos, through smoke and wingbeats and clashing steel, Eldrin felt it. Something vast brushed the edge of the Well.

The air split.

Stone groaned in resistance, the air pulling inward as it had before, gravity bending toward the hollow's heart as dragon speed tore through the cloud cover like a wound reopening. Drakor's twisted wings snapped outward as he dropped toward the Well. Fire bled from the scars along his throat, spilling in erratic bursts that scorched stone and sent nemods scattering.

"DOWN!" Eldrin shouted.

Silverwind veered hard as a blast of warped flame slammed into the ground where they'd been standing moments before. Stone exploded. Heat washed over them, choking and acrid.

Drakor hit the Well like a living catastrophe, forcing the stone to endure him. The impact cracked stone and sent bodies flying. A shockwave tore through the ranks. Dark elves braced and held, but nemods were hurled aside like scraps of smoke. Drakor didn't care. He had come to claim.

But he was not alone.

The sky tore again as a shadow larger than stormlight eclipsed the rim of the Well. Zyressa descended, emerald fire blazing across her chest like a second dawn turned wrong. Rain vaporized around her. Wind fractured against her wings as she chose her landing. Stone bowed beneath her talons as she settled, vast and terrible, wings half-spread as if daring the world to deny her.

Drakor angled lower, circling opposite her, his crooked form cutting sharp arcs through smoke and flame.

Eldrin felt it hit like a second heartbeat. The power of Zyressa's mark. The only way to defeat it was to work as one. "Together!" he shouted, turning Silverwind hard toward Lyria.

She understood before he finished the word. Finnian was already moving as the marks flared, silver meeting blue-white, answering one another in a single rising note.

A current surged upward through the stone beneath their feet, threading through blade, through mark, through breath itself. The air between them brightened, not blinding, but coherent.

Lyria lifted from the ground again, wings catching the updraft of power as she extended one hand toward Eldrin.

Finnian stepped Embermane into the circle without hesitation, and the resonance deepened. "Let's not die today," he muttered.

When the next wave of nemods surged forward, they struck not flesh, but force. Light rippled outward in a widening arc, shattering bone blades, scattering mounts, driving wyverns off their dive path in shrieking confusion. Fire from above broke apart against the edge of the alignment, hissing as it met resistance.

Drakor's eyes narrowed. Zyressa's pupils thinned. For a moment, the Well held. The ground steadied and the circle brightened.

And then the sky shifted again.

Not two shadows this time. More. Much more. Wings beat through the storm banks in uneven cadence, a chaotic rhythm that rolled across the hollow like distant thunder. Dark dragons had answered the Cry. Jagged and hungry, they descended not in formation, but in instinct, spiraling toward dominance.

And the pressure changed. The air thickened, pressing down from every direction at once. The circle flickered, light bending inward under the weight.

Finnian staggered, teeth gritted as the mark at his temples flared. Lyria's wings trembled under the descending force, rattling as heat lashed across them. Eldrin tightened his grip on the dagger, the Aetherstone's pulse beneath them straining to hold alignment as if bracing against a tide.

Zyressa spread her wings fully, fire spilling along their span. A wicked smile curved across her maw. "Break them," she commanded.

The dragons obeyed, and the sky did not merely fall. It descended in fire.

Flame poured from every angle, overlapping streams of heat and ruin, scorching stone, shattering tiers, and forcing the light of the circle inward as darkness pressed from all sides.

And for the first time since the Well aligned, the three friends began to falter. The circle flickered again. Light bent inward beneath the crushing weight of dragonfire from every direction. The alignment wavered as overlapping streams of flame struck from above, from the rim, from the spiraling descent of dark wings.

Finnian gasped as the silver at his temples dimmed, leaving him swaying. Lyria's wings trembled violently, blackening at their tips where heat licked too close. Her mark burned, overloaded. She gritted her teeth and forced the light outward again, but it surged without anchor, strength with nowhere left to land.

Eldrin felt the strain like a blade twisting beneath his ribs. The Aetherstone pulsed beneath the Well's heart, steady, resolute, but its rhythm faltered as the sky thickened with descending mass.

More dragons tore through the clouds. Their shadows overlapped as their roars collided. Heat pressed downward until the stone itself groaned in protest.

Drakor swooped low, twisted wings snapping wide as he exhaled a lance of warped flame that struck the outer edge of the circle. Light shattered outward in sparks as the alignment staggered. He hovered just beyond their failing boundary and lowered his head, fire gathering in his chest. "You feel it, don't you?" he snarled, voice thick with certainty. "The Well isn't answering you anymore." He inhaled, and the world seemed to draw inward with him. "You're mine now."

Eldrin forced himself upright in the saddle, vision blurring as heat distorted the world around him. The dagger felt heavier than iron in his grip. He lifted it anyway. It answered, faintly, but not enough.

Lyria struggled to rise, wings dragging against the stone as her light flickered unevenly at her chest, fierce, defiant, but unanchored.

They were still standing, but they were losing. And Drakor knew it.

Above them, the sky churned, dark, roiling, crowded with wings pressing in from every side. But this time, the Well did not answer.

Chapter 33

Drakor exhaled. Fire tore across the Well in a wild, tearing sweep. Stone screamed as it cracked and split, heat rolling outward in a wave that sent them sprawling.

Finnian and Embermane slammed into a column and barely moved aside as claws raked through the space where his head had been. He came up gasping, blades shaking in his hands, lungs burning with smoke. "This is bad," he rasped, to no one in particular.

Drakor laughed again, louder now, savoring it. "Look at you," he snarled. "So small. So fragile." He reared back, fire gathering again, unstable, furious, more than before.

And then Finnian froze. Not from fear, but from sound. A faint rhythm in the distance. A rhythm beneath the chaos. Felt through the stone beneath Embermane's hooves. Through the mark burning at his temples.

Footsteps.

Hundreds.

No. Thousands.

His breath caught. "Wait," he called.

Eldrin glanced back sharply. "What?"

Finnian lifted his head, eyes unfocused, listening past flame and roar. "They're coming."

And at that exact moment, Fizzlewing burst through smoke and ash, spiraling down in a blaze of gold. His glow was no ember now. It flared bright and fierce, scattering sparks through the dark. "I'm here!" he shouted, voice ringing bright through smoke and flame. "This time I didn't miss!"

The horns sounded. Trumpets blew as they declared arrival.

Drakor wrenched his breath loose. The flames tore free, but not cleanly. They shuddered mid-release, warping as the air buckled around them. Heat fractured into uneven tongues instead of the annihilating sweep he intended.

For the first time, the fire did not obey him.

From the eastern rise, banners broke through smoke, green and silver, vines and leaves entwined. Elven ranks surged down in disciplined formation, shields locked, arrows already darkening the Well in a unified arc.

From the western pass came the answering roar of stone and wind. Drelves. Claws struck rock, wings thundered, and blades flashed in rising light. They converged, and the impact was immediate.

Dark elves faltered. Just a step, just a breath. But it was enough.

Below them, the Well answered as the Aetherstone flared, whole, aligned, and awake. Light rippled outward, not as force, but as connection, threading through the marks, through the dagger, through shield and wing and arrow alike.

Eldrin gasped as the weight in his hand shifted, replaced by clarity. The dagger lit as the Cry swelled again in his chest, no longer solitary, but carried on thousands of voices moving as one.

Warmth surged through Lyria, steady and anchoring. Her wings snapped wide, strength flooding back, not borrowed. Shared.

Finnian staggered as the resonance slammed into him, his marks trembling beneath his skin.

Drakor recoiled, snarling, fire guttering as confusion cut through his triumph. "No," he hissed. "This isn't..." His eyes darted to the banners. To the wings and the unified ranks pressing inward. "This isn't how it's supposed to be!"

And for the first time since shadows had entered the Well, the darkness stopped advancing.

High above the inner ring, Zyressa stilled. The fire along her chest dimmed, not extinguished, but narrowed, sharpening into something focused. Her pupils thinned as the flare from the Well rippled upward, brushing against the mark branded into her scales. The light was no longer fractured. It was joined.

Below her, elves and drelves pressed shoulder to shoulder, blades rising together in disciplined arcs. Arrows flew not in chaos, but in rhythm. Wings beat in formation.

The Cry pulsed again. And far beyond the Well, beyond the battlefield, beyond the reach of fear, it reached something ancient.

Zyressa's claws tightened against the stone, gouging deep furrows into the rim.

A wyvern screamed overhead, banking too sharply as its formation faltered. Another followed, then another, their synchronized dive dissolving into chaos as wings clipped air without purpose.

Nemods and Shadowmanes hesitated mid-strike. One froze, blade half-raised, smoke bleeding from its form as if unsure what shape to hold. Another staggered, clawed feet scraping stone, its head tilting as though listening for an order that never came.

Dark elves faltered. Their ranks wavered, discipline cracking as commands died in throats no longer certain they should be obeyed.

Drakor roared, fury ripping through his chest as fire burst unevenly from his jaws and scorched the ground at his feet. "Move!" he bellowed. "Advance!"

The darkness did not answer.

Eldrin felt the Cry continue, not louder, not sharper, but wider. It moved through the air like memory carried on breath, threading itself into wing and bone and scale.

You are no longer bound.

A wyvern peeled away mid-dive, screeching as it fled skyward. Another turned, not toward the Well, but away from it.

Drakor's eyes widened. "No," he snarled again, stepping forward, wings flaring. "You obey me!"

A nemod dissolved at his feet, its form collapsing inward, smoke unraveling as if the lie holding it together had finally failed.

Lyria felt it in her chest, the pressure easing, the strain lifting. The mark at her neck glowed steady and sure, no longer pushing against resistance.

Eldrin steadied Silverwind as the ground ceased trembling beneath them. The dagger's light no longer flickered. It held, clear, unwavering.

Thalendir stared across the battlefield, disbelief cutting through his focus as a line of dark elves broke ranks and scattered. "They're... stopping," he said.

Drakor backed up a step, then another, fire guttering again as his certainty finally cracked. "This isn't possible," he snarled. "I am their master."

Eldrin lifted his head, voice carrying, not as command, but truth. "No," he said. "Not anymore."

Overhead, the sky shifted and clouds thinned, not burned away, but parted, as if unwilling to obscure what approached.

Silver light broke through first. Gasps rippled through the Well as a massive shape appeared, wings unfolding wide enough to blot out what little light remained. The wind shifted instantly, no longer hot and choking, but sharp and cold, carrying the scent of rain-soaked stone and something older than flame.

"Seralyth," Lyria whispered her name in breath and reverence.

The great white dragon descended without roar or proclamation. Her presence bent the air around her, and the very sky seemed to remember its shape beneath her wings. Her scales caught the fractured light of the Well and returned it multiplied.

Behind her, more dragon shapes emerged, pale and luminous against the bruised sky. Scars marked their hides. Old sorrow lived in their eyes. But they came. And their presence filled the Well with light.

Zyressa faltered mid-dive, not from weakness, but from recognition. The emerald mark across her chest flared in reflex, answering something deeper than rivalry.

Drakor felt it too. And this time, he did not speak.

The Cry of Dragons was no longer divided. It was whole.

And the world remembered why it had once trusted dragonkind at all.

Seralyth did not look at Drakor. Not once.

Her gaze passed over Eldrin first, briefly, with the quiet acknowledgment of something finished. Then she turned to Finnian. She lingered, searching not for power, but for strength. She inclined her head a fraction, the smallest motion imaginable. Finnian exhaled, a breath he hadn't realized he'd been holding.

Then Seralyth looked at Lyria, and her eyes softened as the mark at Lyria's throat warmed in response. "You endured," Seralyth said quietly as the wind shifted around them. "And you remembered."

Lyria's breath caught. She swallowed hard, the memory of exile and battle and grief still burning fresh in her veins. "I didn't do it alone," she said. Her gaze flicked to Eldrin. To Finnian. To the ranks pressing shoulder to shoulder below.

Only then did Seralyth turn her attention to the darkness surrounding her. Every eye was on her. No one had moved since she entered the Well.

Zyressa had landed beside Drakor, the mark pulsing beneath her scales, her gaze fixed on the white dragon. Seralyth approached until they stood nearly eye to eye, something between them that no realm nor history could fully claim. She listened, and the Well listened with her.

And then, very gently, Seralyth's gaze shifted. To Zyressa. To the place where scale met memory. To the mark that was now etched as if it had always been waiting beneath the surface. The third mark. Dragonkind's remembering.

The world inhaled as Seralyth breathed out, slow and reverent. "So," she murmured, eyes locked on Zyressa. "The last one has remembered who she is."

Zyressa lifted her head at last. The fire along her chest steadied, no longer wild.

Drakor shifted beside her, wings tightening, claws scraping stone. "Do not be deceived," he growled. "They would bind you. Use you. As they did before."

Seralyth did not look at him. "You are not bound," she said softly to Zyressa. "You can choose."

The mark pulsed once beneath Zyressa's scales.

Drakor stepped closer. "With you beside me," he said, low and urgent, "dragonkind will rule again. The marks can be taken. The power will be ours."

Seralyth's eyes did not waver. They stayed fixed on Zyressa. "How will you answer?"

Silence stretched across the Well.

Elves and drelves held their ground. Above, dark dragons hovered in uneasy spirals, waiting. The Cry still trembled through the sky. Waiting for an answer.

Zyressa's claws dug deeper into the stone. The emerald mark flared, and for a heartbeat, no one moved.

Drakor made a sound, half snarl, half disbelief. "No," he rasped. "That is not how this works."

Seralyth turned to him then, for the first time. "You are correct," she said. Her gaze returned to Zyressa. "This is how it ends, when fear is no longer obeyed."

The Well did not erupt. It did not blaze. It held. Around them, wings remained folded. Blades remained lowered. The world had not been remade.

But it was no longer being forced to kneel.

The Aetherstone answered, not with light, but alignment. A deep harmony rolled outward from the Well, threading through the three marks as they found one another at last.

Drakor shrieked. Fire tore from his throat in a wild, uneven burst that scorched stone and shadow alike, but the darkness did not surge with it.

It collapsed.

Nemods and their Shadowmanes unraveled where they stood, smoke dispersing as the lie holding them together failed. Wyverns fled, wings beating hard for open sky. Dark elves broke ranks, not routed, but suddenly unsure why they had ever advanced.

Drakor stood alone. "This isn't..." he snarled, voice breaking. "You can't just decide..."

Zyressa finally looked at him. "I just did."

Drakor faltered. Not because he was wounded, but because there was nothing left that would obey him.

The Well grew quiet. And the world, at long last, began to breathe as the sound of many feet rose in unity. Elves and drelves poured around the Well from every arch and rise, ranks interlocking without command, shields lifting instinctively as they closed around the wall and the marked ones. Not to claim them, but to acknowledge them.

Steel stood beside claw. Wing beside leaf. The lie was broken. And the Covenant, long fractured, long denied, stood whole again.

Drakor, ragged, snarling, stripped of dominion, backed into shadow, the hatred he had carried for so long now the only thing left to him.

The shadow panthers emerged without sound.

They circled. Eyes glinting red in the half-light, forms bleeding in and out of the stone itself, creatures born of hunger and command, now unmoored, their purpose hollowed out.

Drakor lashed out, fire bursting in wild, broken arcs. "No," he hissed, backing away. "I made you. You answer to me."

They did not.

They never had.

The first panther leapt. Then another. Claws tore into scale and sinew. Jaws closed around his injured wing, dragging him down as he screamed, not in fury now, but terror. Fire choked out in shattered bursts as the darkness he had unleashed finally claimed him.

And when it was done, there was nothing left to hold them together. The panthers dissolved into smoke and ash, unraveling into nothing as the lie that shaped them failed completely.

The Well fell silent. Not the silence of fear or of waiting. But the silence that follows truth.

Above them, the sky cleared as dragons flew without shadow.

Chapter 34

Lyria stood beside Eldrin, her hand in his, fingers interlaced as if letting go were no longer possible, or necessary. Around them, the world moved in small ways: wounds tended, weapons lowered, voices rising not in cheers but in relief.

Eldrin turned to her slowly, as though afraid sudden movement might wake him from a dream. "I'm glad you remember me," he said.

She nodded, eyes never leaving his face.

He swallowed, something tight easing in his chest at last. "But I would have waited," he said quietly. "As long as it took."

"I know." Her thumb brushed his knuckles. "That's why I came back."

They stood there a moment longer, no urgency, no prophecy pressing them forward. Just two souls who had lost each other and found one another again in a world finally free enough to allow it.

Around them, elves and drelves moved together without hesitation now, sharing water, lifting the fallen, standing side by side. No one commented on it. No one needed to.

Thalendir approached with a rare, unguarded smile. He reached out and clasped Eldrin's shoulder, firm and steady, meeting his gaze without rivalry for the first time in their lives. "Well played, brother," he said. "We just might make a warrior of you yet."

Eldrin studied him. Thalendir's golden hair was completely disheveled, his armor scorched and dented, his features smeared with grime and blood. He laughed softly. "Thanks," he said. "You're a mess."

Thalendir huffed what might almost have been a laugh. "I always have been," he said. Then, quieter, but no less certain, "Good thing you didn't listen to me."

Something long and brittle between them finally gave way.

Eldrin tightened his grip on his brother's arm, not as a prince, not as a rival, but as family. Lyria watched with a gentle smile, understanding exactly what had just been forgiven.

Across the stone, Finnian dropped his hand from his temple with a theatrical groan, rolling his shoulders like an old warrior instead of a young one who had just helped put the world back into balance.

Kaelis watched him for a beat, then crossed her arms. "Does it still hurt?" she asked, gesturing toward his temples.

Finnian shrugged. "Only when the fate of the realms is involved."

She arched an eyebrow. "And when it isn't?"

He grinned, tired, crooked, unmistakably himself. "Then I'm just annoying."

Kaelis studied him a long moment, expression unreadable. "Good."

The word landed lightly. And carried everything.

Above them, the sky continued to clear, not all at once, not perfectly, but enough for sunlight to spill across stone and wing alike. Enough to see one another clearly.

The world did not promise peace. Only balance.

And this time, they were no longer afraid of it.

Chapter 35

High above the broken graveyard, where bone had once marked dominion and memory, wind moved differently now. It did not howl. It simply carried. Clouds drifted low over the mountain ridges, thin and bright, sunlight threading silver through their edges. The air smelled of sunshine and stone and something new, something no longer claimed.

Zyressa stood at the cliff's edge. Below, the drop fell away into open sky. Behind her, small claws scraped against rock. The dragon hatchling hesitated. He was all angles and uncertainty, wings too large for his narrow body, scales still dull with youth. He edged toward the cliff and then back again, talons tapping nervously against stone. The wind tugged at him, and he flattened his wings instinctively.

Zyressa did not move to push him or flare her wings in demonstration. She simply stood beside him, vast and steady, the emerald mark quiet against her chest. Her wings no longer matched its glow. They were pale now, radiant, like light made solid.

The hatchling glanced up at her. "Tell me again about the drelves."

Zyressa followed his gaze toward the distant mountain passes beyond the graveyard. "They are our friends," she said. "And we share the sky with them."

The hatchling tilted his head. "And the elves?" he asked suddenly, peering toward the distant lands where forests met mountains and rivers cut silver lines through green.

"They stand with us," she said. Far below, she could see movement, tiny shapes along roads once divided. Smoke rising from hearths instead of battlefields. "As we stand with them."

For a long moment, the hatchling stood frozen.

Then he leapt.

Not gracefully. Not cleanly. He dropped too fast, wings flailing, body tilting hard to the left. Zyressa stepped forward and launched, not to catch, not to command, but to fly beside him.

The wind caught him properly this time. His wings steadied as he rose higher and higher, riding the updraft. A surprised sound burst from him, half roar, half laughter.

Zyressa banked alongside him, not above, not behind. Equal.

Above them, the sky opened wide and unclaimed. Far off, another shape cut across the horizon, silent, watchful.

Seralyth did not look back, but she smiled.

The halls of the Elven citadel had always carried sound differently. Once, footsteps echoed sharp and precise across the marble floors, measured, deliberate, disciplined. Orders had traveled these corridors like arrows: clean, swift, unquestioned.

Now, the sound was softer. Not weaker. Just different.

King Eldermyst walked without an escort. The banners still hung high, green and silver, embroidered with leaf and crown, but they no longer felt like declarations. They felt like history.

Thalendir walked at his side. Servants paused as they passed, bowing as they always had, but this time the gesture was returned with a nod, not an expectation.

The king stopped before a set of carved doors, ancient oak etched with the decrees of former reigns. Laws burned into memory and wood alike, alongside the names of their ancestors. And those long remembered.

Today, one more would be added.

Eldermyst lifted his hand and rested it against the carving, and for a long moment, he said nothing.

Thalendir did not rush him. “Are you certain?” he asked.

The king's voice, when it came, was quiet. "Yes," he said. "I am done choosing fear."

Eldermyst closed his eyes briefly, not in shame, not in self-defense. In acceptance.

When he opened them again, he turned to the High Scribe standing nearby. "Add it," Eldermyst said, lifting his hand to the carved oak. "Here. Beside his."

The scribe's gaze followed the king's finger. **GANTAR.** The name was freshly cut; the grooves still pale against the darker wood. It had been added the morning after the Well fell silent.

Now there would be another.

The scribe hesitated only a fraction of a breath. "Yes, my king."

Tools were brought forward. The craftsman stepped forward and set his chisel to the wood beside the sage's name. The hammer fell. Measured. Steady.

T-H-A-L-Y-N-D-R-A.

Each strike rang softly through the chamber.

Thalendir watched without speaking, admiration quiet but unmistakable.

When the craftsman stepped back, Eldermyst reached forward. His fingers traced the carved lines, first Gantar.

Then Thalyndra. Now the world would remember what had once been denied.

"And the borders?" Thalendir asked.

Eldermyst nodded once. "They have been opened."

There was no dramatic proclamation. Just gates, long shut, unlocked.

Far below the citadel, guards stepped aside as elven hands met drelven claws at the threshold. Thalendir watched from the balcony as the first of the mountain drelves entered openly through the main road instead of the hidden passes. "They will test us," he said.

"They should," Eldermyst replied. A pause. "And we will answer differently."

Thalendir glanced at his father, not as heir, not as rival, but as a son who had learned the cost of silence. And what it takes to forgive.

Below, an elfling stopped in the road to stare up at a pair of folded wings. The drelf crouched to meet its gaze, not wary, not guarded. Curious.

The king exhaled slowly. He understood that the citadel did not change in a day, and the forest did not forget overnight. But something rigid had loosened.

And in its place, choice reigned.

Outside the drelf kingdom, on a broad stone terrace carved into the mountainside, Kaelis stood with a long drelf spear balanced lightly in her grip. Finnian stood opposite her, trying very hard to look competent.

Kaelis stepped forward and demonstrated. Her movement was fluid, powerful, tail adjusting her balance with effortless precision as she pivoted through the throw. The spear cut clean through the air and struck the target dead center with a satisfying crack. She did not look impressed with herself. She simply retrieved it. "Your turn," she said, matter-of-fact.

Finnian inhaled deeply. "Right. Simple."

He launched the spear. It left his hand with enthusiasm. Too much enthusiasm. He over-rotated. The spear clipped the training circle, ricocheted sideways, and embedded itself, quivering, into a decorative pillar carved with ancestral names.

Silence.

Kaelis stared at the pillar. "You throw like an elf," she said flatly.

Finnian straightened. "I am an elf."

"Exactly."

Lyria bit her lip to suppress a smile as she leaned against the stone railing beside Eldrin. He crossed his arms, expression carefully neutral.

Finnian rubbed the back of his neck. "I was testing the wind."

"There is no wind."

"Then I was testing destiny," he said, throwing up his hands.

Kaelis stepped closer and wrenched the spear free from the wounded pillar. "Try again."

She repositioned his grip. Adjusted his elbow and tapped his shoulder into alignment. "Less hope. More balance."

He tried again. This time the spear struck the outer ring.

Kaelis nodded once. "Better."

Finnian beamed like he had just sung the world back into harmony.

Lyria failed to contain it this time. She laughed, bright and unguarded.

Eldrin murmured under his breath, "He'll get it, eventually."

"I know," Lyria replied softly.

Above them, on a higher ledge overlooking the terrace, Nyxari stood. She watched correction offered without insult, pride shared instead of guarded, and laughter rise where exile once lived.

The wind shifted and brushed across her face. "The future rarely arrives as we imagine it," she said quietly.

Below, Finnian attempted another throw. This time it struck dead center. His triumphant shout echoed across the stone.

Nyxari's lips curved faintly. "Sometimes, it's kinder."

Epilogue

Fizzlewing liked the quiet best, especially after everything had stopped trying to fall apart. The Shrouded Vale shimmered as it always had, with pools reflecting skies that never quite matched the world beyond, and leaves whispering to one another about things they had seen and would never tell.

Fizzlewing drifted lazily through a shaft of light, his wings humming as he trailed motes of gold that vanished almost as soon as they appeared. Everything was where it should be. That had taken some doing.

He landed on the edge of the Revealing Pool and peered in, his head tilting slightly. The water no longer showed battles. No fire. No broken wings or falling stars. Only paths. Open ones.

"See?" he murmured to the Pool. "Told you they'd figure it out."

The Pool did not answer. It never did when things went right.

Fizzlewing's gaze drifted not forward, but back, following the long threads of choice and fear that had led to this moment. He remembered a silver-haired king standing alone beneath ancient trees, carrying three names in his heart and believing he could save only two of them.

Believing exile was mercy. Believing silence was protection. Believing a kingdom could survive a wound sealed too tightly.

He had been wrong. At last, he knew it. Not as guilt, but as truth.

Fizzlewing watched that understanding take root, not as self-punishment, but as acceptance of what had been lost and what could no longer be undone.

Love, once denied, does not vanish. It waits.

Forgiveness had not come to the king because his choices were justified. It came because he had finally stopped defending them.

Someone had helped him reach that place. A quiet hand on the scale. A voice that asked nothing in return. A wise old sage.

Gantar had always believed that truth, once faced, required not punishment, but courage. His final gift had not been power, or prophecy, or even absolution.

It had been permission. Permission to lay down the lie. To grieve without excuse. To let love, speak at last.

His sacrifice had been enough.

Fizzlewing smiled, small and private. That was how forgiveness always came, when the last lie left the room and nothing remained but what was real.

He flitted closer to the Pool and caught a glimpse of the Well far away, quiet now and whole. Three marks at rest. Dragons choosing the sky for themselves. Elves and drelves walking the same roads without counting steps.

Balance. Not perfect, but honest.

"That'll do," Fizzlewing said, satisfied.

He lifted off again, looping once through the Vale's golden light before darting toward a hidden passage only the Vale remembered.

There were other doors to watch. Other paths to nudge. But at least this time, no one was lost.

If you enjoyed this book, please take a moment to write a review.

Every review is important, and it will help others find my books (so I can keep writing in this series).

Thanks for your help!

C. Star

Coming soon...

A new fantasy series by C. Star

When a broken dragon chooses a rider no one believes in, neither of them will ever be the same again.

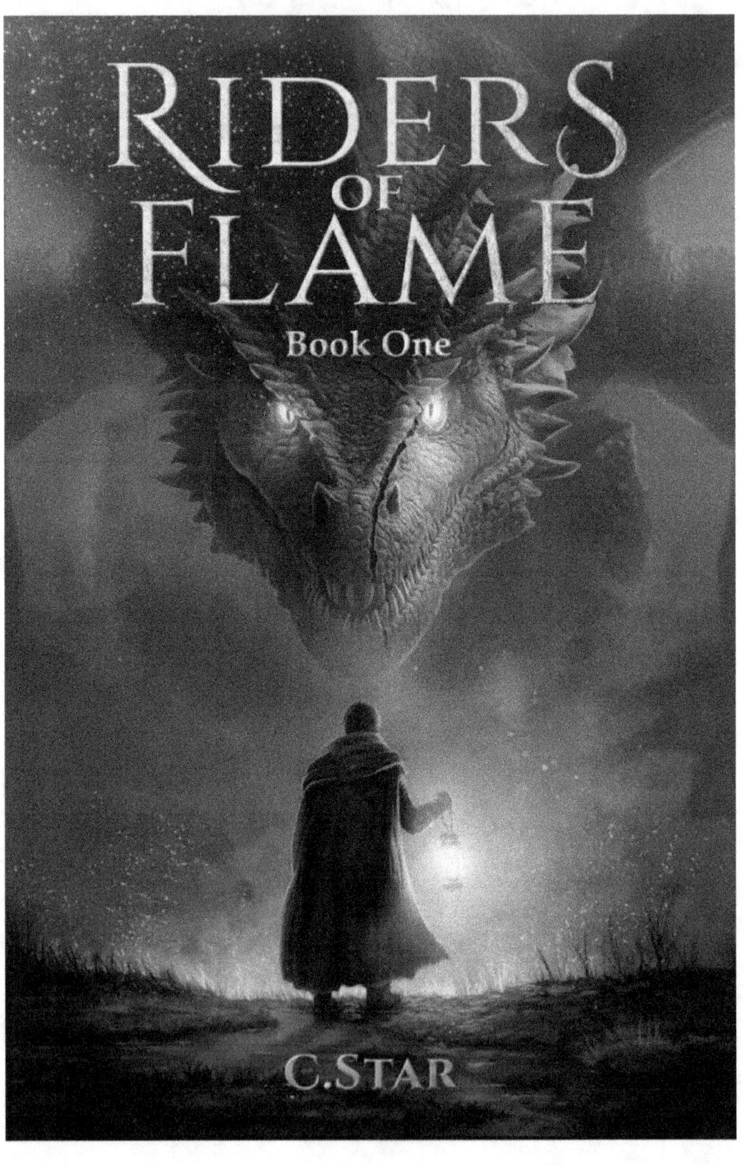

Join my mailing list to receive the latest news about my books (and extra goodies!)

Community:

Mail: Cynastar019@gmail.com

My Website: Cstarbooks.com

Signup for Newsletter:

https://cstarbooks.com/#newsletter

Thank you for reading my books!

Character & Creature Guide

Main Characters

- **Lyria Ironwing** ***(LEER-ee-uh)*** — Drelf mark-bearer, part dragon, part elf.
- **Eldrin** ***(ELL-drin)*** — Elven warrior, son of King Eldermyst.
- **Finnian** ***(FIN-ee-an)*** — Elf. Eldrin's loyal friend.
- **Gantar** ***(GAN-tar)*** — Elven sage and healer.
- **Thalendir** ***(THAL-en-deer)*** — Elf. Eldrin's older brother, son of King Eldermyst.
- **King Eldermyst** ***(ELL-der-mist)*** — King of the Elves, father to Eldrin and Thalendir.
- **Kaelis Skythorn (KAY-liss SKY-thorn)** — Drelf. Lyria's fiercely loyal best friend from the Drelf Kingdom.
- **Orendir** ***(OR-en-deer)*** — Elf. High Warden to King Eldermyst.
- **Nyxari the Veilkeeper (NICK-sar-ee) —** Drelf seer who interprets visions of fate and prophecy. Keeper of ancient lore tied to the marks.
- **Seralyth** ***(SERR-uh-lith)*** — Ancient white dragon.
- **Thariel** ***(THAR-ee-el)*** — Elf. Eldrin's mother.

- **Fizzlewing** ***(FIZZ-uhl-wing)*** — Mischievous pixie guide from the Shrouded Vale.

Elven Council

- **Lady Alariel** ***(AH-lar-ee-el)*** — Mistress of Lore.
- **Lord Thalion** ***(THAL-ee-on)*** — Commander of the Elven Guard.
- **Elder Faelorn** ***(FAY-lorn)*** — Master of Nature.
- **Lady Seraphina** ***(SERR-uh-fee-nuh)*** — Ambassador of Alliances.
- **Elder Sylthir** ***(SILL-theer)*** — The Shadow Watcher.

Horses

- **Silverwind** ***(SILL-ver-wind)*** — Eldrin's mare.
- **Duskrunner** ***(DUSS-kruhn-er)*** — Gantar's gelding, ridden by Lyria.
- **Embermane** ***(EM-ber-mayn)*** — Finnian's buckskin gelding.
- **Steel** ***(STEEL)*** — Thalendir's black stallion.

Creatures

- **Nemods (NEH-mods)** — Abyss-born horrors of shadow and flame. Their cracked hides glow with molten veins, their ember eyes burning with soulless hunger. Once bound to dragon kind, they now serve Vartharax and his lieutenant, Drakor.

- **Varagos**: Nemod commander, Drakor replaced Skalvorr with him in Book One.
- **Wyverns (WHY-vernz)** — Winged, reptilian beasts smaller than dragons but no less fierce.
- **Shadowmanes (SHAD-oh-mayns)** — Nightmarish steeds forged of shadow and fire, ridden by nemods into battle. Their blackened hides cling to skeletal frames, hooves carving scorched trenches as they ride. Eyes burning like molten glass, their silent gallop carries the echo of nightmares through the dark.
- **Shadow Panthers (SHA-doh PAN-thurz).** — Stealth-born predators woven of smoke and sinew. Once forest guardians, they were corrupted by Vartharax's darkness. Their eyes burn amber-red, their claws cut like obsidian, and when slain—after several strikes, for they move through both flesh and spirit—they dissolve into mist, leaving only silence and ash behind.
- **Aetherstone (AY-ther-stone)** — An ancient relic of power, said to guide its bearer when all light is lost.
- **Gladehorn (GLAYD-horn)** — Watcher of Balance in the drelf realm. A reindeer-like guardian with silver-dappled fur, spiraled antlers that glow at dusk, and calm, water-clear eyes.
- **Skitterling (SKI-tur-ling)** — Small, swift creatures with foxlike faces and green-gold hides feathered

along their wings and tails. Once used by dragons as spies and decoys, they were nearly hunted to extinction by their own masters.

- **Gravorn (GRAH-vorn)** — A giant and ally to the drelves. Stoic and bound by oath, he aids Lyria's war-band in the battle against Drakor, embodying ancient strength and loyalty.
- **Tree Sage** — Ancient, sentient spirit of the Arden's roots who aids Lyria and her allies by opening hidden paths.

Dragons

- **Zyressa (ZAI-ress-uh)** — A fierce green dragon, scarred by battle and quick to challenge those who cross her.
- **Korrath (KOR-ath)** — A crimson dragon of immense power and pride, longtime rival of Drakor.
- **Drakor (DRAY-kor)** — Twisted lieutenant of Vartharax. Smaller than most of his kind but more cunning, he wields shadow and deceit as weapons.
- **Vartharax (VAR-thuh-raks)** — The Dark Dragon Lord who broke the ancient Covenant and commands the nemods.
- **Velthar (VELL-thar)** — A rogue bronze-scaled dragon who conspires with Zyressa for his own gain.

- **Rhaegorath (RAY-goh-rath)** — The black dragon bound to Camyra's will, summoned through dark magic to serve her command.

More Elves

- **Master Trainer Aldareth (AL-dah-reth) —** Veteran weapons master of the Elven Guard and mentor to Eldrin. In Book Two, he leads the spies that Gantar sends into the Arden.
- **Caelith (KAY-lith) —** Skilled elven warrior who trains and patrols with Eldrin in Book One. In Book Two, he serves as one of Gantar's spies under Aldareth's command.
- **Aelar (AY-lar) —** Quiet, sharp-eyed spy sent by Gantar to accompany Aldareth on the mission into the Arden.
- **Dareth (DARE-eth) —** Scout who patrolled the Elven borders in Book One and fought to protect the realm's outer forests.
- **Erynder (AIR-in-der) —** Veteran Elven scout who fought beside King Eldermyst to defend the drelf kingdom. In Book Two, he remains behind to aid the drelves, joining Lyria's war-band and scouting the Umbrin alongside Seliora.
- **Aerion (EYE-ree-on)** — Calm and precise female elven archer, unmatched with a bow. In Book Two,

she serves among Gantar's spies sent with Master Aldareth into the Arden. In Book Two, she serves among Gantar's spies sent with Master Aldareth into the Arden.

- **Seliora (Seh-lee-OR-ah) —** Red-haired, emerald-eyed female elf who fought beside King Eldermyst to defend the drelf kingdom. Remaining behind to aid the drelves, she later joins Lyria's war-band, scouting the Umbrin alongside Erynder before the battle.

Dark Elves/Umbrin/Nightborn

- **Drovane (DROH-vayn) —** Leader of the Umbrin, the dark elves. His serpent-smooth voice and black eyes conceal centuries of ambition and deceit.
- **Camyra (KAH-mih-rah) —** The golden-haired enchantress aligned with the dark elves. Her allure masks a dangerous will; she commands the black dragon Rhaegorath through forbidden magic.
- **Vaelrys (VAY-liss) —** Female commander chosen by Drovane for her skill and intellect.

More Drelves

Zeynar (ZAY-nar) — Drelf warrior sent by Nyxari to guide Master Trainer Aldareth and the Elven spies through the Arden to the Umbrin camp.

About the Author

C. Star grew up in rural Nebraska, the youngest of three and the only girl—taunted and teased by her older brothers, which she's convinced made her fierce, determined, and full of stories worth telling.

She wrote her first book at ten years old and hasn't stopped since. From early stories scribbled in notebooks to award-winning song lyrics written on a whim, storytelling has always been in her bones.

After writing in other genres under the name Cynthia Star, she followed her heart into young adult fantasy—where magic awakens, dragons rise, and unlikely heroes dare to change the world.

C. Star now lives in New Mexico, where she hikes the desert foothills with her dog, River, collects odd-shaped rocks, and dreams up new worlds with every step.

You can check out all my books on Amazon by Cynthia Star

(know a young person who likes dragons?)

The Beepy Bumpy Blue Bug ~ picture book (ages 2-6)

What Color is Your Dragon? ~ picture book (ages 4-8)

The Moonlit Dragon ~ picture book (ages 4-8)

The Dragon Flyers Book One ~ (ages 7-10)

The Dragon Flyers Book Two ~ (ages 7-10)

The Dragon Flyers Book Three ~ (ages 7-13)

The Dragon Flyers Book Four ~ (ages 8-13)

Happiness Came with a Cat (New Edition) ~ Adult memoir/self-help

#1 Amazon Best Seller - Starving, Bingeing, Purging ~ Adult memoir/self-help

www.ingramcontent.com/pod-product-compliance
Lightning Source LLC
LaVergne TN
LVHW020710110826
845149LV00012B/2202
* 9 7 9 8 9 9 5 5 9 9 3 0 2 *